# THE LA CHANCE MINE MYSTERY

# THE LA CHANCE MINE MYSTERY

## S. CARLETON
### (SUSAN MORROW JONES)

INTRODUCTION BY KARL WURF

**WILDSIDE PRESS**

Originally published in 1920.
Published by Wildside Press, LLC.
Visit us online at wildsidepress.com.

# INTRODUCTION

## KARL WURF

S. Carleton was the pen name of Susan Morrow Jones (1864–1926), a Canadian novelist from Halifax, Nova Scotia. She also published under the names Helen Milecete and Carleton-Milecete, which allowed her to reach different audiences while exploring varied literary themes. Her use of multiple signatures was not unusual for the time and reflected both marketing strategy and creative freedom.

Jones came from a literary family and was part of a network of Maritime women writers active around the turn of the twentieth century. Her sister, Helen Morrow Paske Duffus, also wrote fiction, and her cousin Alice Jones (writing as Alix John) became known for novels and travel literature. These connections gave Susan Morrow Jones a place in the small but significant Canadian literary scene of her era.

Her work often bridged two worlds: the familiar landscapes of Canada and the cultural currents of Britain. In novels such as *A Girl of the North: A Story of London and Canada*, which she wrote as Helen Milecete, she wove together domestic life, travel, and questions of identity. Readers found in her work a blend of regional color and cosmopolitan perspective, reflecting the mobility and shifting loyalties of her generation.

Jones's novels sit at the crossroads of Edwardian popular fiction and early Canadian regional literature. She was skilled at taking elements familiar from British adventure and mystery writing—hidden fortunes, perilous travel, and unexpected revelations—and reshaping them with Canadian settings and concerns. Wilderness landscapes, harsh climates, and frontier labor were not simply backdrops in her stories but active forces influencing character and plot.

*The La Chance Mine Mystery* is a prime example of this style. The story uses the mining frontier as a stage for intrigue, mixing the suspense of hidden motives with the realities of wilderness travel and work. Jones knew how to pair atmosphere with action, creating briskly paced narratives that kept readers turning pages while also rooting them in Canadian soil.

Influences on her style likely came from the adventure tradition of writers such as Arthur Conan Doyle and H. Rider Haggard, as well as from the regional realism of her Canadian peers. This combination of mystery structure and local detail gave her books both popular appeal and lasting cultural significance.

If you are interested in exploring more of her work, several other titles stand out. As Helen Milecete: *A Girl of the North*, *Out of Drowning Valley*, and *The Forest Runner*. As S. Carleton: *The Career of Mrs. Osborne*. As Carleton-Milecete: *A Detached Pirate: The Romance of Guy Vandeleur*.

# CHAPTER 1

## I COME HOME: AND THE WOLVES HOWL

*I am sick of the bitter wood-smoke,*
*And sick of the wind and rain:*
*I will leave the bush behind me,*
*And look for my love again.*

Little as I guessed it, this story really began at Skunk's Misery. But Skunk's Misery was the last thing in my head, though I had just come from the place.

Hungry, dog-tired, cross with the crossness of a man in authority whose orders have been forgotten or disregarded, I drove Billy Jones's old canoe across Lac Tremblant on my way home to Dudley Wilbraham's gold mine at La Chance, after an absence of months. It was halfway to dark, and the bitter November wind blew dead in my teeth. Slaps of spray from flying wave-crests blinded me with gouts of lake water, that was oddly warm till the cutting wind froze it to a coating of solid ice on my bare hands and stinging face, that I had to keep dabbing on my paddling shoulder to get my eyes clear in order that I might stare in front of my leaky, borrowed canoe.

To a stranger there might have seemed to be nothing particular to stare at, out on a lake where the world was all wind and lumpy seas and growing November twilight; but anyone who had lived at La Chance knew better. By the map Lac Tremblant should have been our nearest gold route to civilization, but it was a lake that was no lake, as far as transport was concerned, and we never used it. The five-mile crossing I was making was just a fair sample of the forty miles of length Lac Tremblant stretched mockingly past the La Chance mine toward the main road from Caraquet—our nearest settlement—to railhead: and that was forty miles of bad water, sown with rocks that were sometimes visible as tombstones in a cemetery and sometimes hidden like rattlesnakes in a blanket. For the depth of Lac Tremblant, or its fairway, were two things no man might ever count on. It would fall in a night to shallows a child could wade through, among bristling needles of rocks no one had ever guessed at; and rise in a morning to the tops of the spruce scrub on its banks—a sweet spread of water with not a rock to be seen. What hidden spring fed it was a mystery. But in the bitterest winter it was never cold enough to freeze, further than to form surging masses of frazil ice that would neither let a canoe push through them, nor yet support the weight of a man. Winter or summer, it was no thoroughfare—and neither was the ungodly jumble of swamp and mountains that stopped me from tapping the lower end of it—or I should not have spent the last three months in making fifty miles of road through untrodden bush to Caraquet, over which to transport the La Chance gold to a post-road and a railway: and it was no chosen return route of mine to La Chance now, either.

If I could draw you a map I should not have to explain the country. But failing that I will be as clear as I can.

The line of Lac Tremblant, and that of the road I had just made from Caraquet to La Chance, ran away from each other in two sides of a triangle—except that the La Chance mine was five miles down the far side of the lake from Caraquet, and my road had to half-moon round the head of Lac Tremblant to get home—a lavish curve, too, by reason of swamps.

But it was on that half-moon road that I should have been now, if my order to have a horse meet me at the Halfway stables I had built at the beginning of it had not been forgotten or disregarded by someone at La Chance.

Getting drenched to the skin with lake water was no rattling good exchange for riding home on a fresh horse that felt like a warm stove under me, but a five-mile short cut across the apex of the road and lake triangle was better than walking twenty-two miles along the side of it on my own legs—which was the only choice I had had in the matter.

I was obliged to get home, for reasons of my own; but when I walked in on Billy Jones, the foreman at the Halfway stables, that afternoon, after months of absence and road-making, there was not even a team horse in his stables, let alone my own saddle mare. There was not a soul about the place, either, but Billy himself, blandly idle and sprawling over a grubby old newspaper in front of the stove in his shack.

His welcome was heartening, but his intelligence was not. No one had told him a word about me or my mare, he informed me profanely; also that it was quite impossible for me to ride over to La Chance that night. There were not any work horses at the Halfway, because he had doubled up the teams for some heavy hauling from Caraquet, according to my orders sent over from Caraquet the week before, and no horses had been sent back from La Chance since. He guessed affably that someone might be driving over from the mine in the morning, and that after tramping from Caraquet I had better stay where I was for the night.

I hesitated. I was dog-tired for once in my life, but I had not done any tramp from Caraquet that day, if I had told the bald truth. Only I had no idea of telling it, nor any wish to explain to Billy Jones that I had been making a fool of myself elsewhere, doing a solid week of hospital nursing over a filthy boy I had found on my just-finished road the morning I had really left Caraquet. From the look of him I guessed he had got hurt cutting down a tree and not getting out of the way in time, though he was past telling me that or anything else. But I had also guessed where he lived, by the dirt on him, and was ass enough to carry him home to the squalid, half-French, half-Indian village the Caraquet people called Skunk's Misery.

It lay in the bush, in a slanting line between Caraquet and Lac Tremblant: a nest of thriftless evil stuck in a hollow you might pass within twenty yards of, and never guess held a house. Once there I had no choice but to stay and nurse the boy's sickening pain, till his mother came home from some place where she was fishing eels for the winter; for none of the rest of the population of fat-faced, indifferent women—I never saw a man, whether they were away in the lumber woods or not—would lay a hand on him. I will say plainly that I was more than thankful to hand him over to his mother. I had spilt over myself a bottle of some nameless and abominable brew that I'd mistaken for liniment, and my clothes smelt like carrion; also the lean-to I had lived in was so dirty that I scratched from suspicion all day long, except when I was yawning from a week of hardly closing my eyes. Altogether, as I said, I was dog-tired, if it were not from walking, and I might have stayed at Billy Jones's if I had not been crazy to get rid of my dirt-infected clothes. The worst reek had gone from them, but even out in the open air they smelt. I saw Billy Jones wrinkle up his nose to sniff innocently while he talked to me, and that settled me.

"I have to get home," I observed hastily. "Wilbraham expected me a week ago. But I don't walk any twenty-two miles! I'll take your old canoe and a short cut across the lake."

I was the only man who ever used Lac Tremblant, and the foreman of the Halfway stables cast a glance on me. "If it was me, I'd walk," he remarked drily. "But take your choice. The lake's a short cut right enough, only I wouldn't say where *to*—in my crazy old birchbark this kind of a blowing-up evening!"

That, and a few more things he said as he squinted a weather-wise eye on the lake, came back to me as I fought his old canoe through the water. And fighting it was, mind you, for the spray hid the rocks I knew, and the wind shoved me back on the ones I didn't know. Also the canoe was leaking till she was dead logy, and the gusts were so fierce I could not stop paddling to bail her. The short, vicious seas that snapped at me five ways at once were the color of lead and felt as heavy as cold molasses. But, for all that, crossing Lac Tremblant was saving me twenty-two miles on my feet, and I was not wasting any dissatisfaction on the traverse. Only, as I shoved the canoe forward, I was nearer to being played out, from one thing on top of another, than ever I was in my life. I pretended the paddle that began to hang in spite of me was only heavy with freezing spray and that the dead ache in my back was a kink. But I had to put every ounce there was in my six feet of weary bones into lightning-change wrenches to hold the old canoe head on to the splattering seas and keep her from swamping. I was very near to thinking I had been a fool not to have stayed with Billy Jones—when I was suddenly aware of absolute, utter calm in the air that felt as warm on my face as if I'd gone into a house; of tranquil water under the forefoot of the canoe that had jumped forward under me as the resistance of the wind ceased; and of the lake shore—dark, featureless, silent—within twenty feet of me. I was across Lac Tremblant and in the shelter of the La Chance shore!

There is no good in denying that for five minutes all I did was to sit back and breathe. Then I lit my pipe, that was dry because it was inside my shirt; bailed the unnecessary water out of the canoe and the immediate neighborhood of my legs; and, without meaning to, turned a casual eye on the shore at my right hand.

It might have been because I was tired, but that shore struck me as if I had never seen it before; and on a November evening it was not an inviting prospect. Bush and bush, and more bush, grew down to the very verge of the water in a mass that spoke of heavy swamp and no landing. Behind that, I knew, was rising land, country rock, and again swamp and more swamp—and all of it harsh, ugly, and inhospitable. But the thought that came over me was that it was more than inhospitable: it was forbidding. High over my head poured the bitter wind in a river of sound through the bare tree tops; close at hand it rustled with a flurry of dead leaves that was uncannily like the bustle of inimical businesses pursued insolently in the dark, at my very elbow; and suddenly, through and over all other sounds, there rose in the harsh gloom the long, ravening cry of a wolf.

Heaven knows I was used to the bush, and no howling was much to me; but you know how things come over you sometimes. It came over me then that I was sick of my life at La Chance; sick of working with Wilbraham and sicker still of washing myself in brooks and sleeping on the ground—for I had not been in a house since August. Before I knew it I was speaking out loud as men do in books, only it was something I had thought before, which in books it generally isn't: "Scott, I'm a fool to stay here. I'd sooner go and work on day's wages somewhere and have a place *to go home to!*" And then I felt my face get red in the dark, for I knew what I meant, if you do not.

There was nothing to go home to at Wilbraham's, except a roof over my head, till circumstances sent me out into the bush again. In the daytime there were the mine and the mill. At night there was the bare living room of Wilbraham's shack, without a book, or a paper, or a decent chair; Wilbraham himself, fat, pig-headed, truculent, stumping the devil's sentry-go up and down the bare floor, talking eternally about himself and the mine, till a saint must have loathed the two of them; Thompson, the mine superintendent, silent, slow and stupid, playing ghastly solitaire games in a corner with a pack of dirty cards; and me, Nick Stretton, hunching myself irritably on a hard chair till I could decently go to bed. Even the bush was better than night after night of that—and suddenly I felt my thoughts bursting out, even if I had sense enough to keep my mouth shut.

I was as sick of the bush as I was of the shack. I wanted a place of my own and a life of my own: and I was going to have it. There was nothing but old friendship to tie me to Wilbraham's; I could do as well anywhere else, and I was going there—tomorrow; going somewhere, anyhow, so that when my day's work was over I could go home to a blazing fire on a wide hearth, instead of Wilbraham's smelly stove where no one ever cleaned the creosote out of the pipe—and where the girl I had had in my head for ten years would be waiting for me.

Don't imagine it was any girl I knew that I was thinking of; it was just a dream girl I meant to marry, when I found her. I'd never met such a girl anywhere, and it sounds like a fool to say I knew I was going to meet her: that she was waiting somewhere in the world for me, just as I was looking for her. I knew exactly what she must be like. She would have that waving bronze-gold hair that stands out in little separate, shining tendrils; eyes that startled you with their clear blue under dark, level eyebrows—I never look twice at a girl with arched brows—the rose-white, satin-smooth skin that goes with all of them, and she would move like— Well, you've seen Pavlova move! Her voice—somehow one of the most important things I knew about her seemed to be her voice—would be the clear, carrying kind that always sounds gay. I was certain I should know my dream girl—first—by that. And that was the girl—I forgot it was all made-up child's play—who somewhere in the world was waiting for me, Nick Stretton; a fool with nothing on earth but six feet of a passably good body, and a dark, high-nosed face like an Indian's, who was working in the bush for Wilbraham instead of sieving creation for her. Well, I would start tomorrow; and, where the clean heavens meant me to, I should find her!

And with the words I came alive to the dark lake, and the leaky canoe I sat in, and the knowledge that all I had been thinking about a bronze-haired girl was just the cracked dream of a lonely man. Even if it had not been, and I could have started to look for a real girl tomorrow, I had to get back to Wilbraham's tonight. My drenched clothes were freezing on me, and I was hungrier than the wolf who had just howled again, as I picked up my slippery paddle and started for the La Chance landing.

There was no light there, naturally, since no one ever used the lake except myself, and I had been away for months; but as I rounded the point between the canoe and the landing, and slipped into the dark of its shadow, the lamplight from Wilbraham's living room shone out on me in a narrow beam, like a moon path on the water. As I crossed it and beached the canoe I must have been in plain sight to anyone on the shore, though all I saw was the dark shingle I stepped upon. I stooped to lift the canoe out of water—and I did what you mean when you say you nearly jumped out of your skin.

Touching my shoulder, her hand fiercely imperative in the dark, was a girl—at La Chance, where no girl had ever set foot!—and she was speaking to me with just that golden, carrying voice I knew would belong to my own dream girl, if she were keeping it down to a whisper.

"So you're here," was what she said; and it would have fitted in with the fool's thoughts I had just come out of, if it had not been for her tone. That startled me, till all I could do was to nod in the dark I could just see her in. I could not discern what she looked like, for her head was muffled in a shawl; and I never realized that all she could see of me was my height and general make-up, since my face must have been invisible where I stood in the shadow.

"You!" her golden voice stabbed like a dagger. "I won't have you staying here—where I am! I told you I'd speak to you when I could, and I'm speaking. You kept your word and disgraced me once, if I don't know how you did it; but I won't run the chance of *that* again! I'm safe here, except for you; and you've got to let me alone. If you don't, I—I—" she stammered till I knew she was shaking, but she got hold of herself in the second. "You won't find it safe to play any tricks with the gold here—or me—if that's what you came for," she said superbly, "and you've given me a way to stop it. *That's* why I've sneaked out to meet you: not because I care for you. You must go away, or—I'll tell that you're here! Do you hear? I don't care what promises you make me—they always came easily to you. If you want me to hold my tongue about you, you've got to go. Go and betray me, if you like—but *go!*"

There was dead, cold hatred in it, the kind a woman has for a man she once cared for, and it staggered what wits I had left. I nodded like a fool, just as if I had known what she was talking about, and went on lifting the canoe ashore. Whether I really heard her give a terrified gasp I don't know; perhaps I only thought so. But as I put the canoe on the bank I heard a rustle, and when I looked up she was gone. There was nothing to tell me she had really even been there. It was just as probable that I was crazy, or walking in my sleep, as that a girl who talked like that—or even any kind of a girl—should be at La Chance. The cold, collected hatred in her voice still jarred me, since it was no way for even a dream girl to speak. But what jarred me worse was that the whole thing had been so quick I could not have sworn she had been there at all. I was honestly dazed as I walked up the rough path to Wilbraham's and my shack. I must have stood in front of it a good five minutes, with my wet clothes freezing as hard as a board, and the noise of the men in the bunk house down by the mine coming up to me on the night wind.

"'If I be I, as I should be, I've a little dog at home, and he'll know me,'" I said to myself at last like the old woman in the storybook, only with a grin. For when I went into the house there would be the neglected living room with the smelly stove, and Wilbraham walking up and down there as usual; and Dudley Wilbraham's conversation would bring any man back to his senses, even if he needed it worse than I did. I opened the shack door and went in—and in the bare passage I jerked up taut.

The living room faced me—and there was no stove in it. And no Wilbraham, walking up and down and talking to himself. There was a glowing, blazing log fire in a stone fireplace that must have been built while I was away; and, sitting alone before it, exactly as I had always thought of her, was my dream girl—that I had meant to hunt the world for to welcome me home!

# CHAPTER 2

## MY DREAM: AND DUDLEY'S GIRL

All I could do was to stand in the living room doorway and stare at her.

There she sat by the fire, in a short blue skirt that showed her little feet in blue stockings and buckled shoes, and a blue sweater whose rolling collar fell away from the column of her soft throat. And she was just exactly what I had known she would be! There was a gold crest to every exquisite, warm wave of her bronze hair; her level eyebrows were about five shades darker, and her curled-up eyelashes darker still, where she sat with her head bent over some sort of sewing. And even before she looked up and I saw her eyes, the beauty of her caught me at my heart. I had never thought even my dream girl could be as lovely as she was. But there was more to her face than beauty. It was so young and sweet and gay, and—when you looked hard at her—so sad, that I forgot I ought either to speak up or go away. Of who she was or how she came to be at La Chance, I had no earthly clue. I knew, of course, that it was she who had met me at the landing, and common sense told me she had taken me for someone else: but I had no desire to say so, or to go away either. And suddenly she looked up and saw me.

Whoever she was she had good nerves, for she never even stared as women do at a strange man. I could have been no reassuring vision either, standing there in moccasined feet that had come in on her as silently as a wolf or an Indian; with dirty, frozen clothes; and a face that the Lord knows is dark and hard at its best, and must have been forbidding enough that night between dirt and fatigue. But that girl only glanced at me as quietly as if she had known I was there.

"Did you— Were you looking for anyone?" she asked. And the second I heard her voice I knew she guessed she had spoken to me a quarter of an hour ago in words she would probably have given all she possessed to prevent a stranger from knowing she had need to speak to anyone.

Only that was not the reason I half stammered, "Not exactly." It was because I could see her eyes—and they were like sapphires, and the sea, and the night sky with the first stars in it. I snatched off my cap that I had forgotten, and bits of melting ice fell off it and tinkled on the floor. The sharp little sound brought my wits back to me. Perhaps I had never really thought my dream girl would come true, but once I had found her I never meant to lose her. And I knew, if I cared a straw for my life and the love that was to be in it, that I must meet her now *for the first time*; that nothing, not even if she told me so herself, must make me admit she had come to me at the lake by mistake, or that I had ever heard her voice before.

I said, easily enough, "I'm afraid I startled you. I'm Stretton, Wilbraham's partner"—which I was to the extent of a thousand dollars—"I've just come home."

And crazy as it sounds, I felt as if I had come home, for the first time in my life. For the girl of my dreams came to her feet with just that lovely, controlled ease you see in Pavlova, and with the prettiest little gesture of welcome.

"Oh, you're frozen stiff," she said with a kind of dismayed sympathy. "And I heard Mr. Wilbraham say someone had forgotten to send out your horse for you, and that you'd probably walk—the whole way from Caraquet! You must be tired to death. Please come to the fire and get warm—now you've come home!"

I thought of the peculiar smell that clung to my stained old coat and the company I had kept at Skunk's Misery—though if I had guessed what that wretched boy was going to mean to me I might have grudged my contact with him less—and I would not have gone near my dream girl for a fortune. "I think I'll get clean first," I began, and found myself laughing for the first time in a week. But as I turned away I glanced back from the dark passage where Charliet, the French-Canadian cook, was supposed to keep a lamp and never did, and saw the girl in the living room look after me—with a look I had never seen in any girl's eyes, if I'd seen a hunted man have it.

"Gad, she knows I know she met me—and she doesn't mean to say so," I thought vividly. What the reason was I couldn't see, or whom there could be at La Chance that such a girl should find it necessary to tell that she would not have him disgrace her, and that he must go away. It made me wrathy to think there could be anyone she needed to hit out at like that. But we had a strange lot at the mine, including Dunn and Collins, a couple of educated boys who had not been educated enough to pass as mining engineers, and had been kicked out into the world by their families. It might have been either of those two star failures in the bunk house. The only person it could not have been was Dudley Wilbraham; since aside from the fact that she could easily speak to him in the shack she could not have told him he must go away from his own mine. Which reminded me I'd never even asked where Dudley was or one thing about the mine I'd been away from so long.

But my dream girl, where no girl had ever been, was the only thing I could think of. I had meant to get some food and go to bed, but instead I threw my Skunk's Misery clothes out of the window, and got ready to go out to supper and see that girl again. Who under heaven she could be was past me, as well as how she came to be at La Chance. I would have been scared green lest she was the wife of some man at the mine, only she had no wedding ring on the slim left hand that had beckoned me to the fire. Yet, "She can't just be here alone, either, and I'm blessed if I see who she can have come with," I thought blankly. And I opened my room door straight on Marcia Wilbraham—Wilbraham's sister!

"*Well*," I said. It was the only thing that came to me. I knew immediately, of course, that the girl in the living room must have come out with Marcia; but it knocked me silly to see Marcia herself at La Chance. I had known Marcia Wilbraham, as I had known Dudley, ever since I wore blue serge knickerbockers trimmed with white braid. She never went anywhere with Dudley. She had money of her own, and she spent it on Horse Show horses, and traveling around to show them. But here she stood in front of me, in a forsaken backwoods mine that I should not have expected even Dudley himself to stay at if I had not known his reasons.

"I don't wonder you say 'well,'" Marcia returned crisply. She was good-looking in a big way, if you did not mind brown eyes that were too small for her face and a smile that showed her gums. I had never liked or disliked her especially, any more than you do any girl about your own age whom you've always known. "I've been here for three months! I was very near going home a month ago—but I don't think I'll go now. I believe I'll try a winter here."

"A winter!" I thought of Marcia "trying a winter," and I laughed.

"Oh, you needn't throw back your handsome Indian head to grin at me, Nicky Stretton," said she crossly. "I'm tired of always doing the same thing. And anyhow, the stable lost money, and I had to sell out!"

"But why stay here—with Dudley?" I let out. The two of them had always fought like cats.

"I'm going to do some shooting—and wolf hunting," Marcia smiled the ugly smile I never could stand. "I'm going to stay, anyhow; so you'll have to bear it, Nicky!"

"I'm—charmed!" I thought like lightning that my dream girl would do whatever Marcia did, and I blessed my stars she was staying; though I knew she would be all kinds of a nuisance if she insisted on turning out to hunt wolves. She was all but dressed for it even then, in a horrid green divided skirt that made her look like a fat old gentleman. But it was not Marcia I meant to talk about.

"Have you brought the—other girl—to hunt wolves, too?" I inquired, as we moved on down the passage; there was no upstairs to the shack.

"No," said Marcia quite carelessly, if I had not caught the snap in her eyes. "She's come to hunt Dudley! She's going to marry him."

"She's *what?*" I was suddenly thankful we had left the light from my open door and that Charliet despised keeping a lamp in the passage. The bland idea that I had found my dream girl split to bits as if a half-ton rock had landed on it. For her to be going to marry anyone was bad enough; but *Dudley*, with his temper, and his drink, and the drugs I was pretty sure he took! The thing was so unspeakable that I stopped short in the passage.

Marcia Wilbraham stopped short too. "I don't wonder you're knocked silly," she said. "Here, come out of this; I want to speak to you, and I may as well do it now!" She pushed me into the office where Dudley did his accounts—which was his name for sitting drinking all day, and never speaking to anyone—and shut the door. "Look here, Nicky, if you're thinking that girl is a friend of mine, she isn't! I don't know one thing about her. Except that this summer I had reason to oblige Dudley, and one day he came to me—you know he was in New York for nearly two months—"

I nodded. I had not cared where he was, so that he was away from La Chance, where he and old Thompson would drive a tunnel just where I knew it was useless.

"Well, he came to me in the first of August, and said he was going to marry a girl called Paulette Brown—and he wanted me to bring her out here! Why he didn't marry her straight off and bring her out here himself, I don't know; he only hummed and hawed when I asked him. But anyhow, I met Paulette Brown, *for the first time*, at the station, when we started up here—she and I and Dudley. And she puzzled me from the second we got into the Pullman, and I saw her pull off the two veils she'd worn around her head in the station! And she puzzles me worse now."

"Why?" I might have been puzzled myself, remembering Paulette Brown's speech to me in the dark, but it was none of Marcia's business.

"Because I know I've seen her before," Marcia returned calmly, "only with no 'Paulette Brown' tacked on to her. I've seen her dance somewhere, but I can't think *where*—and that's the first thing that puzzles me."

"I don't see why," I said disagreeably, "considering that everyone dances somewhere all day long just now."

"It wasn't that kind of dancing. It was rather—wonderful! And there was some story tacked on to it," Marcia frowned, "only I can't think what! And the second thing that puzzles me about Paulette Brown—I tell you, Nicky, I believe she can't *bear* Dudley, and that she doesn't want to marry him!"

It was the first decent thing I had heard from her, and I could have opened my mouth and cheered. But I said, "Then why's she here?"

"Just because it suits her for some reason of her own," Marcia was earnest as I had never seen her. "Nicky, I don't think she's anything in the world but some sort of an adventuress—only what I can't understand about her is what she wants of Dudley! It isn't money, for I know he's tried to make her take it, and she wouldn't. Yet I know, too, that she hadn't a cent coming up here, and she hasn't now—or even any clothes but summer things, and a blue sweater she wears all the time. She never speaks about herself, or where she comes from—"

"I don't see why there should be any mystery about that!" It was a lie, but I might not have seen, if she had not spoken to me incomprehensibly in the dark. "Dudley probably knows all about her people."

"A girl called Paulette Brown doesn't have any people," scornfully. "Besides, her name isn't Brown, or Paulette—she used to forget to answer to either of them at first; and if Dudley knows what it really is, I'm going to know too—before I'm a month older! I tell you I've seen her before, and I know there was some kind of an ugly story tacked on to her and her dancing. That, and her real name, are up in the attic of my brain somewhere, and some day they'll come down!"

"Well, they won't concern me," I cut in stolidly. Whoever Paulette Brown was, if she were going to marry Dudley Wilbraham ten times over, she was the one girl in the world who belonged to me—and I was not going to have her discussed by Marcia behind a shut door.

But Marcia's retort was too quick for me. "They may interest you, all the same, if that girl's what I think she is! Don't make any mistake, Nicky; she's no chorus girl out of work. She's a lady. Only—she's been something else, too! You watch how she uses a perfectly trained body."

I all but started. I had seen it already, when I thought she moved like Pavlova. "Anything else?" I inquired disagreeably.

"Yes," said Marcia quietly. "She's afraid for her life, or Dudley's—I can't make out which. Wait, and you'll see. Come on; we'll be late for supper. It would have been over hours ago if Dudley and I hadn't been out shooting this afternoon. We've only just come in."

But I was not thinking about supper. The Wilbrahams had been out, and Paulette Brown, left alone, had taken her chance to speak to someone. That she had happened to mistake her man and spoken to me made no difference in the fact, and it came too aptly on Marcia's suspicions about her. But "My good heavens, I won't care what she did," I thought fiercely. My dream girl's eyes were honest, if they were deep blue lakes a man might drown his soul in, too. If she were Dudley's twice over I was going to stand by her, because by all my dreams of her she was more mine. "I haven't time, or chances, to be watching pretty ladies," I said drily, "and I wouldn't bother over it myself if I were you. I'd let it go at plain Paulette Brown!"

"If you could," said Marcia, just as drily. And over her words, close outside the window, a wolf howled.

It startled me, as it had startled me once before that evening, only this time I knew the reason. "Scott, I never knew the wolves to be coming out so early in the season!" I was thankful to be back to things I could exclaim about. "And down here, beside the house, I never saw any!"

"No; so Dudley said," Marcia returned almost absently. She opened the door for herself, because I had forgotten it, and stood looking at the lighted living room at the end of the passage by the front door. "But the wolves have been round for a week—that was what I meant when I said I was going to have some wolf hunts! The mine superintendent's going to take me."

"Thompson!" I let out. Then I chuckled. Marcia was likely to have a great wolf hunt with Thompson, who knew no difference between a shotgun and a rifle, and would have legged it from a fox if he had met it alone. "Marcia Wilbraham, I'll pay you five dollars if you ever get out wolf hunting with Thompson. Why, the only thing he *can* do for diversion is to play solitaire!"

"Oh, him—yes," said Marcia carelessly and without grammar. "But I didn't mean old Thompson. He's been gone for a month, and we've a new man. His name's Macartney, and he's been here two weeks."

It was news to me, if it was also an example of the way Dudley Wilbraham ran his mine. But before I could speak Marcia nodded significantly down the passage to the living room door. I had been looking into the room myself, as you do at the lighted stage in a theatre, and I had seen only one thing in it: my dream girl—whose name might or might not be Paulette Brown, whom Dudley Wilbraham had more right to than I had—sitting by the fire as I had left her, that fire I had dreamed I should come home to, just myself alone, and talking to Dudley. But Marcia had been looking at something else, and now my gaze followed hers.

A tall, lean, hard, capable-looking man stood on the other side of the fire. He was taking no share in the conversation between Dudley and the girl who had only lived in my dreams till tonight. He was watching the living room door, quite palpably, and it struck me abruptly that I had not far to seek for Marcia Wilbraham's reason for staying the winter at La Chance. But I might have taken more interest in that and in Macartney, the new mine superintendent, too, if the girl sitting by the fire had not seen Marcia in the doorway and risen to her feet.

For she floated up, effortlessly, unconsciously, to the very tips of her toes, and stood so—like Pavlova!

# CHAPTER 3

## DUDLEY'S MINE: AND DUDLEY'S GOLD

*I have stared my eyes blind for her,*
*Bridled my body alive for her,*
*Starved my soul to the rind for her—*
  *Do I lose all?*
                                    —The Lost Lover.

I could feel Marcia's satisfied, significant smile through the back of my neck as I shook hands with Dudley and was introduced in turn to Miss Brown—the last name for her, even without the affected Paulette, though I might not have thought of it but for Marcia—and to Macartney, the new incumbent of Thompson's shoes. Dudley, little and fat, in the dirty boots he had worn all day, and just a little loaded, told me to wait till the morning or go to the devil, when I asked about the mine. Charliet banged the food on the table for supper—Marcia despised housekeeping, and if the living room had been reformed nothing else had—and I sat down in silence and ate. At least I shovelled food into my famished stomach. My attention was elsewhere.

Paulette Brown sat beside Dudley. She was just twice as pretty as I had realized, even when the first sight of her struck me dumb. Her eyes were as dark as indigo, in the lamplight, and a marvellous rose color flitted in her cheeks as she spoke or was silent. She had wonderful hands, too, slim and white, without a sign of a bone at the wrists; but I had a curious feeling that they were the very strongest hands I had ever seen on a girl. Remembering Dudley, it hurt me to look at her; and suddenly something else hurt me worse, that I had been a fool not to have thought of before. Macartney, the mine superintendent, was new there; I knew no more of him than I did of Paulette Brown—not so much, perhaps, thanks to Marcia—and it came over me that he might have been the man for whom she had taken me tonight, and that it was he she had crept out into the dark to speak to in secret. I looked at him over my coffee cup, and there was something about him I did not like.

He was a tall man, very capable-looking, as I said; extremely fair and rather handsome, with hard, grayish eyes that looked straight at you when he spoke. He had a charming laugh—yet when he laughed I saw suddenly what it was that I did not like about him; and it was nothing more nor less than a certain set look about his eye muscles. Some gamblers have it, and it did not strike my fancy in the new mine superintendent at La Chance. But watch as I might, I saw no sign of an understanding between him and my dream girl. It was impossible to be sure, of course, but I was nearly sure. She spoke to him as she spoke to Marcia and Dudley—she never addressed one word to me— just easily and simply, as people do who live in the same house. Macartney himself talked mostly to Marcia, which was no business of mine. Only I was somehow curiously thankful that it had not been Macartney whom Paulette had meant to meet in the dark. There was something about his eyes that said he was no safe customer for any girl to speak to with hatred—especially a girl whom another girl was watching, as Marcia was watching Paulette Brown. I decided it must have been either Dunn or Collins—our two worthless Yale boys at the mine—whom she had wanted to get rid of, and I felt better; for it would be easy enough to save her trouble by doing that myself. They might just have come back to La Chance like me, for all I knew, because Dudley had a trick of sending the men heaven knew where to prospect.

It was rot, anyhow, to be taking a girl's affairs so seriously. I looked at my dream girl's clear eyes, and thought that if she knew what Marcia and I were thinking about her she might have good reason to be angry. Also that Dudley probably knew all about her evening stroll and what she was doing at La Chance, if Marcia did not. And Dudley's self-important voice cut through my thoughts like a knife:

"Where on earth were you this evening, Paulette?" he was demanding irritably. "I couldn't see a sign of you when Marcia and I went out, and you weren't anywhere when we came in!"

"I don't know"—the girl began—and I saw the color go out of her face, and it made me angry.

"I can tell you where Miss Brown was," I said deliberately, "if she's ashamed to own it. She was good and settled by this fire."

Why I lied for her I could not say. But the glance she turned on me gave me a flat sort of feeling, as if Marcia might be right and she was there for reasons of her own that I had all but stumbled on by accident. I was a fool to care; but then I had been a fool all day with my silly thoughts of leaving La Chance to chase the world for an imaginary girl, and more fool still to think I had found her there waiting for me. I said something about being tired and went off to bed. I was tired, right enough, but I was something else too. All that business about the girl I meant to find and marry may sound like a child's silly game to you, but it had been more than a game to me. It had been a solid prop to hold to in ugly places where a man might slip if he had not clean love and a girl in his head. And now, at seven-and-twenty, I wanted my child's game to come true: just my own fire, and my own girl, and a life that held more than mere slaving for money. And it had come true, as far as the fire and the welcome home; only the girl was another man's.

I knew what I ought to do was to get out of La Chance, but I could not screw myself up to the acceptance of the obvious fact that there were other girls in the world than Paulette Brown. I told myself I was too dead tired to care. I stumbled to my window to open it—Charliet's lamp had burned out while I was at supper and the room was stifling—and a sudden odd sense that someone or something was under my window made me stand there without raising it. And there was some *thing*, anyway. The windows in the shack were about a yard above the ground. There was a glimpse of the moon through the wind-tortured clouds, now on the rough clearing, now on the thick spruces round the edge of it—for my window looked on the bush, not toward the bunk house and the mine. And as the moonlight flickered back on the clearing I saw my clothes I had worn at Skunk's Misery and tossed out for Charliet to burn because they smelled—and something else that made me stare in pure surprise.

There was a wolf—gaunt, gray, fantastic in the moonlight—rolling on my clothes; regardless of the human eyes on him and within ten feet of the house. It was so crazy that I almost forgot the girl Marcia had said was only "called" Paulette Brown. I jerked up the window and stood waiting for the wolf to run. And it did not take the least notice of me. I could have shot it ten times over, but the thing was so incredible that I only stood staring; and suddenly my chance was gone. The beast picked up my coat, as a dog does a bone, and disappeared with it like a streak into the black bush.

"Scott, I never saw a wolf behave like that!" I thought. But one more impossibility in an impossible day did not matter. I left the window open and tumbled into bed.

I would have forgotten the thing in the morning, only that when I got up *all* my Skunk's Misery clothes had disappeared, and Charliet had not taken them, because I asked him. I did not mention last night's wolf to him, because I was in a hurry to catch Dudley and tell him I meant to leave La Chance. But I did not tell him, for when I thought of leaving my dream girl to him it would not come to my tongue. An obstinate, matter-of-fact devil got up in my heart instead and prompted me to stay just where I was. I looked at Dudley—little, fat, pompous, and so self-opinionated that it fairly stuck out of him—and thought that if I had a fair chance I could take my dream girl from him. I might be dark as an Indian and without a cent to my name except the few dollars I had sunk in the mine, but I did not drink or eat drugs; and I knew Dudley did one and guessed he did the other. Interfering with him was out of the question, of course; it was not a thing any man could do to his friend, deliberately. I supposed he would be good to the girl, according to his lights. But, all the same, I decided to stay at La Chance. I saw Dudley was brimming over with something secret, and I hoped to heaven it was not his engagement, and that I should not have to stand my own thoughts of a girl translated into Dudley's. But he did not mention her. He hooked his fat wrist into my elbow and trotted me down to the mine.

It was an amateur sort of mine, as you may have gathered. Dudley had no use for expert assistance or for advice. And it was a simple looking place. The shore of Lac Tremblant there ran back flat to a hill, a quarter of a mile from the water, with a solid rock face like a cliff. Along that cliff face came first Dudley's shack, then Thompson's tunnel, then—a good way farther down—the bunk house, the mill, and a shanty Dudley called the assay office. But I stared at a new hole in the cliff, farther down even than the assay office.

"Why, you've driven a new tunnel," I exclaimed.

"Yes, my young son," said Dudley; and then he burst out with things. Macartney had run that new tunnel as soon as he came and struck quartz that was solid for heaven knew how far, and carrying thick, free gold that assayed incredibly to the ton. The La Chance mine, whose name had been more truth than poetry—for when I made fifty miles of road that cost like the devil, to haul in machinery and a mill it was pitch and toss if we should ever need it—had turned out a certainty while I was away.

I stood silent. It meant plenty to me, who had only a trifle in the thing, but I was the only soul in the world who knew what it meant to Dudley. Stocks, carelessness, but chiefly bull-headed extravagance, had run through every cent he had, and La Chance had saved him from having to live on Marcia's charity—if she had any. There was no fear, either, of his being interfered with in the bonanza he had struck; for leaving out my infinitesimal share, Dudley was sole owner—and he had bought a thousand acres mining concession from the Government for ten dollars an acre, which is the law when a potential mining district in unsurveyed territory is more than twenty miles by a wagon road from a railway. All he had to do with would-be prospectors was to chuck them out. He had got in ten stamps for his mill over the road I had built from Caraquet, and—since Macartney arrived—was milling stuff whose net result made me stare, after the miserable, two-dollar ore old Thompson had broken my heart with.

"So you see, we're made," Dudley finished simply. "Macartney struck his vein first go off, and we'll be able to work it all winter. You'd better start in today and get some snowsheds built along the face of the workings—they ought to have been started a week ago. Why in the devil"—drink and drugs do not make a man easy to work with, and you never knew when Dudley might turn on you with a face like a fiend—"didn't you get back from Cara-quet before? You'd nothing to keep you away this last week!"

"I'd plenty," I returned drily. "And I may remind you that I didn't pro-pose to have to walk back!" It was the first time I had mentioned my missing horse. I did not mention my stay in Skunk's Misery: it was a side show of my own, to my mind, and unconnected with Dudley—though I ought to have known that nothing in life is ever a side show, even if you can't see the door from the big tent.

"Oh, your horse," said Dudley more civilly. "I didn't think I'd forgotten about it, but I suppose I must have. I was a good deal put out getting Thomp-son off."

"What happened about him?" I had had no chance to ask before.

"Oh, I never could stand him," and I knew it was true. "Sitting all the evening playing cards like a performing dog! And he wasn't fit for his work, either. I told him so, and he said he'd go. He went out to Caraquet nearly a month ago—I thought you knew. D'ye mean you didn't see him going through?"

I shook my head. It was a wonder I had not, for I had spent most of last month fussing over some bad places on the road, by the turn where I had found my boy from Skunk's Misery, and I ought to have seen Thompson go by. But the solution was simple. There was one Monday and Tuesday I had my road gang off in the bush, on the opposite side from the Skunk's Misery valley, getting stuff to finish a bit of corduroy. In those two days I could have missed seeing Thompson, and I said so.

"You didn't miss much," Dudley returned carelessly. "This Macartney's a long sight better man."

"Where'd you get him?" I was pretty sure it was not Macartney for whom my dream girl had mistaken me in the dark, but there was no harm in knowing all I could about him.

Dudley knocked the wind straight out of my half suspicion.

"Thompson sent him," he returned with a grin. "I told him to get some-body. Oh, we parted friends all right, old Thompson and I! He saw, just as I did, that he wasn't the man for the place. Macartney struck that vein first go off, and that was recommendation enough for me. But here's Thompson's, if you want to see it!" He extracted a folded letter from a case.

It was written in Thompson's careful, back-number copperplate, perhaps not so careful as usual, but his unmistakably. And once and for all I dis-missed all idea that it could have been Macartney who was tangled up with Paulette Brown. Old Thompson's friends were not that sort, and he vouched for knowing Macartney all his life. He was a well-known man, according to Thompson, with a long string of letters after his name. Thompson had come on him by accident, and sent him up at once, before he was snapped up elsewhere.

"Thompson seems to have got a move on in sending up his successor," said I idly. "When did he write this?" For there was no envelope, and only Montreal, with no date, on the letter.

"Dunno—first day he got to Montreal, it says," carelessly. "Come along and have a look at the workings. I want you to get log shelters built as quick as you can build them—we don't want to have to dig out the new tunnel mouth every time it snows. After that you can go to Caraquet with what gold we've got out and be gone as long as you please. Now, we may have snow any day."

I nodded. The winter arrives for good at La Chance in November, and besides the exposed tunnel mouth, there was no shelter over the ore platform at the mill. This year the snow was late, but there was no counting on that. And I blinked as I went out of the white November sunshine into Macartney's new tunnel, and the candlelight of his humming stope. One glance around told me Dudley was right, and the man knew his business; and it was the same over at the mill. It seemed to me superintendent was a mild name for Macartney, and general manager would have fitted better. But I said nothing, for Dudley considered he was general manager himself. Another thing that pleased me about the new man was that he seemed to be doing nothing, till you saw how his men jumped for him, while Thompson had never been able to keep his hands off the men's work. There was none of that in Macartney; and if he had struck me as capable the night before he looked ten times more so now, as he placidly ran four jobs at once.

He was a good-looking figure of a man, too, in his brown duck working clothes, and I did not wonder Marcia Wilbraham had taken a fancy to him. Dudley would probably be blazing if he caught her philandering with his superintendent, but it was no business of mine. And anyhow, Macartney had my blessing since it could not be he to whom Paulette Brown had meant to speak the night before. That ought to have been none of my business either, and to get it out of my head I turned to Dudley, fussing round and talking about tailings. And one omission in all he and Macartney had shown me hopped up in my head. "Where's your gold?" I demanded.

"That's one thing we don't keep loose on the doorsteps," Macartney returned drily, and I rather liked him for it, since he knew nothing of my share in the mine.

But Dudley snapped at him: "Why can't you say it's in the house—in my office? Stretton's going to take it into Caraquet; there's no sense in making a mystery to him. Come on, Stretton, and have a look at it now!" He stuck his fat little arm through mine, and we went back to the house by the back door and Charliet's untidy kitchen. It was the shortest way, and it was not till afterwards that I remembered it was not commanded by the window in his office, like the front way. I was not keen on going; later I had a sickly feeling that it was because I had a presentiment of seeing something I did not want to see. Then all I thought was that I had a hundred other things to do, and though I went unwillingly, I went.

"The gold's in my safe, in boxes," Dudley said on the way, "and that I'm not going to undo. But I've a lump or two in my desk I can show you."

"Lying round loose?" I shrugged my shoulders.

"No, it's locked up. But no one ever comes in here but me, and"—he gave a shove at the office door that seemed to have stuck—"and Miss Brown!"

But I was speechless where I stood behind him. There was the bare office; Dudley's locked desk; Dudley's safe against the wall. And turning away from the safe, in her blue sweater and blue skirt and stockings and little buckled shoes, was my dream girl!

Something in my heart turned over as I looked at her. It was not that she had started, for she had not. She just stood in front of us, poised and serene, and some sort of a letter she had been writing lay half finished on Dudley's desk. But something totally outside me told me she had been writing no letter while we were out; that she knew the combination of the safe; had opened it; had but just shut it; and—*that she had been doing something to the boxes of gold inside it.*

There was nothing in her face to say so, though, and my thought never struck Dudley. He gave her a nod and a patronizing: "Well, nice girl," without the least surprise at seeing her there. But I had seen a pin dot of blue sealing wax on the glimpse of white blouse that showed through the open front of her sweater, and something else. I stooped, while Dudley was fussing with the lock of his desk, and picked up a curious little gold seal that lay on the floor by the safe.

Whether I meant to speak of it or not I don't know; for quick as light, the girl held out her hand for it. I said nothing as I gave it to her. Dudley did not see me do it; and, of course, it might have been a seal of his own. But, if it were, why did not Paulette Brown say so—or say something—instead of standing dead white and silent till I turned away?

I knew—as I said "Oh" over Dudley's gold, and my dream girl slipped out of the room—that I had helped her to keep some kind of a secret for the second time. And that if she had any mysterious business at La Chance it was something fishy about Dudley's gold!

# CHAPTER 4

## THE MAN IN THE DARK

It sounded crazy, for what could a girl like that do to gold that was securely packed? But women had been mixed up in ugly work about gold before, and somehow the vision of my dream girl standing by the safe stuck to me all that day. Suppose I had helped her to cover up a theft from Dudley! It was funny; but the ludicrous side of it did not strike me. What did was that I must see her alone and get rid of the poisonous distrust of her that she, or Marcia, had put into my head. But that day went by, and two more on top of it, and I had no chance to speak to Paulette Brown.

Part of the reason was that I had not a second to call my own. La Chance had been an amateur mine when we began it, and it was one still. There was only Dudley—who did nothing and was celebrating himself stupid with drugs, or I was much mistaken—Macartney, and myself to run it; with not enough men even to get out the ore, without working the mill and the amalgam plates. It had been no particular matter while the whole mine was only a tentative business, and I had been having half a fit at Dudley's mad extravagance in putting up a ten-stamp mill when we had nothing particular to crush in it. But now, with ore that ran over a hundred to the ton being fed into the mill, and Macartney and I doing the work of six men instead of two, I agreed with Dudley when he announced in a sober interval that we required a double shift of men and the mill to crush day and night, instead of stopping at dark—besides a cyanide plant and a man to run it.

But Macartney unexpectedly jibbed at the idea. He returned bluntly that he could attend to the cyanide business himself, when it was really needed; while as to extra men he could not watch a night shift at the plates as well as a day one, and he would have to be pretty sure of the honesty of his new amalgam man before he started in to get one. Also—and it struck me as a sentiment I had never heard from a mine superintendent before—that if we sent out for men half of those we got might be riffraff and make trouble for us, without so much as a sheriff within a hundred miles. "I'd sooner pick up new men one at a time," he concluded, "even if it takes a month. We've ladies here, and if we got in a gang of tramps—" he gave a shrug and a significant glance at Dudley.

"Why, we've some devils out of purgatory now," I began scornfully, and stopped—because Dudley suddenly agreed with Macartney. But the waste of time in making the mine pay for itself and the stopping of the mill at night galled me; and so did the work I had to do from dawn to dark, because any two-dollar-a-day man could have done it instead.

Macartney seemed to be made of iron, for he took longer hours than I did. But he could talk to Marcia Wilbraham in the evenings, while Dudley stood between me and the dream girl I thought had come true for me when first I came to La Chance.

I watched her, though; I couldn't help it. There were times when I could have sworn her soul matched her body and she was honest all through; and times when a devil rose up in me and bade me doubt her; till between work and worry I was no nearer finding out the kind she really was than to discovering the man she had meant to speak to in the dark the night she blundered on me. Yet I had some sort of a clue there, if it were not much of one. Dunn and Collins, our two slackers who had been kicked out of Yale to land in our bunk house, evidently had some game on. Dunn I was not much bothered about: he was just a plain good-for-nothing, with a perennial chuckle. But Collins was a different story. Tall, pale, long-eyelashed, his *blasé* young face barely veiled a mind that was an encyclopædia of sin—or I was much mistaken. And he and Dunn had suddenly ceased to raise Hades in the bunk house every night and developed a taste for going to bed with the hens. At least, the snoring bunk house thought so. If they went abroad instead on whatever they were up to, I never caught them at it; but I did catch them watching *me*, like lynxes, whenever they were off shift. I never saw either of them speak to Miss Brown, but I got a good growing idea it was just Collins she had meant to interview the night she spoke to me: and it fitted in well enough with my doubts about her and Dudley's gold, for I would have put no gold stealing past Collins. As for Paulette Brown herself, I could see no earthly sense in Marcia's silly statement that "she was afraid for her life—or Dudley's." She was afraid *of* Dudley, I could see that; for she shrank from him quite often. But on the other hand, I saw her follow him into his office one night, when he was fit for no girl to tackle, and try to get him to listen to something. From outside I heard her beg him to "please listen and try to understand"—and I made her a sign from the doorway to come away before he flew at her. I asked her if there were anything I could do, and she said no; it was only something she wanted to tell Dudley. But suddenly she looked at me with those clear eyes of hers. "You're very—good to me," she said rather piteously.

I shook my head, and that minute I believed in her utterly. But the next night I had a jar. I was starting for Caraquet the morning after, with the gold Dudley had in his office, so I was late in the stable, putting washers on my light wagon, and came home by a short cut through the bush, long after dark. If I moved Indian-silent in my moccasins it was because I always did. But—halfway to the shack clearing—I stopped short, wolf-silent; which is different. Close by, invisible in the dark spruces, I heard Paulette Brown speaking; and knew that once more she was meeting a man in the dark, and, this time, the right one! I could not see him any more than I could hear him, for he did not speak; but I knew he was there. I crouched to make a blind jump for him—and my dream girl's voice held me still.

"I don't care how you threaten me: you've got to *go*," she said doggedly. "I know I've my own safety to look after, but I'll chance that. I'll give you one week more. Then, if you dare to stay on here, and interfere with me or the gold or anything else, I'll confess everything to Dudley Wilbraham. I nearly did it last night. I *won't* trust you—even if it means your giving away my hiding place to the police!"

Whoever she spoke to moved infinitesimally in the dark. He must have muttered something I could not hear, for the girl answered sharply: "As for that, I'm done with you! Whether you go or don't go, this is the last time I'll ever sneak out to meet you. When you dare to say you love me"—and once more the collected hatred in her voice staggered me, only this time I was thankful for it—"I could die! I won't hear of what you say, remember, but I'll give you one week's chance. Then—or if you try anything on with me and the gold—I'll tell!"

There was no answer. But my blood jumped in me with sheer fury, for answer or no answer, I knew who the man beside her was. Close by me I heard Dunn's unmistakable chuckle: and where Dunn was Collins was too. I behaved like a fool. I should have bounced through the bush and grabbed Dunn at least, which might have stopped some of the awful work that was to come. But I stood still, till a sixth sense told me Collins was gone, just as I could have gone myself, without sound or warning. Yet even then I paused instead of going after him. First, because I had no desire to give my reason for dismissing him next morning; second, because I had a startling, ghastly thought that I'd heard Macartney's quiet, characteristic footstep moving away—and if a hard, set-eyed man like our capable superintendent had been out listening to what a girl said to Collins, as I had, I didn't know how in the devil I was to make him hold his tongue about it. And in the middle of that pleasant thought my dream girl spoke again, to herself this time: "Oh, I can't trust him! I'll have to get hold of the gold myself—at least all I've marked."

On the top of her words a wolf howled startlingly, close by. It was evidently the last touch on what must have been a cheerful evening, for Paulette Brown gave one appalled spring and was gone, fleeing for the kitchen door. I am not slow on my feet. I was in the front way before she struck the back one. From the front door I observed the living room, and what I saw inside it before I strolled in there made me catch my breath with relief and comforting security for the first time that night. Macartney could not have been out listening in the dark, if I had. He sat lazily in the living room, talking to Marcia, with his feet in old patent leather shoes he could never have run in, even if it had not been plain he had not been out-of-doors at all. Marcia had evidently not been spying either, which was a comfort; and Dudley was out of the question, for he dozed by the fire, palpably half asleep. But suddenly I had a fright. The girl who entered the living room five minutes behind me had very plainly been out; and I was terrified that Marcia would notice her wind-blown hair. I spoke to her as she passed me. "You're losing a hairpin on the left side of your head," was all I said. And much I got for it. My dream girl tucked in her wildly flying curl with that sleight of hand women use and never even looked at me. But the thing was done, and I had covered up her tracks for the third time.

I decided to fire Collins before breakfast the next morning and get off to Caraquet straight after. But I didn't; and I did not fire Collins, either. When I went to the bunk house and then to the mine, where he was a rock man, he had apparently fired himself, as Paulette had told him to. He was nowhere to be found, anyhow, or Dunn either. I wasted an hour hunting for him, and after that Macartney wanted me, so that it was late afternoon before I could load up my gold and get off. And as I opened the safe in Dudley's office I swore.

There were four boxes of the stuff; small, for easy handling; and if I had had time I would have opened every hanged one of them. Even as it was, I determined to do no forwarding from Caraquet till I knew what something on them meant. For on each box, just as I had expected even before I heard Paulette Brown say she had marked them, was a tiny seal in blue wax!

The reason for any seal knocked me utterly, but I couldn't wait to worry over it. No one else saw it, for I loaded the boxes into my wagon myself, and there was nobody about to see me off. Dudley was dead to the world, as I'd known he was getting ready to be for a week past; Marcia, to her fury, had had to retire to bed with a swelled face; and Macartney was the only other person who knew my light wagon and pair of horses was taking our clean-up into Caraquet—except Paulette Brown!

And there was no sign of her anywhere. I had not expected there would be, but I was sore all the same. I had helped her out of difficulties three times, and all I'd got for it was—nothing! I saw Macartney coming up from the mill, and yelled to him to come and hold my horses, while I went back to my room for a revolver. This was from sheer habit. The snow still held off, and before me was nothing more exciting than a cold drive over a bad road that was frozen hard as a board, a halt at the Halfway stables to change horses, and perhaps the society of Billy Jones as far as Caraquet—if he wanted to go there. The only other human being I could possibly meet might be someone from Skunk's Misery, though that was unlikely; the denizens of Skunk's Misery had few errands that took them out on roads. So I pocketed my gun mechanically. But as I went out again I stopped short in the shack door.

My dream girl, whom I'd never been alone with for ten minutes, sat in my wagon, with my reins in her hands. "My soul," I thought, galvanized, "she can't be—she must be—coming with me to Caraquet!"

# CHAPTER 5

## THE CARAQUET ROAD:
## AND THE WOLVES HOWL ONCE MORE

*Why comest thou to ride with me?*
*"The road, this night, is dark."*
*Dost thou and thine then side with me?*
*"Ride on, ride on and hark!"*
—The Night Ride.

There she sat, anyhow, alone except for Macartney, who stood at the horses' heads. Wherever she was going, I had an idea he was as surprised about it as I was, and that he had been expostulating with her about her expedition. But, if he had, he shut up as I appeared. I could only stammer as I stared at Paulette, "You—you're not coming!"

"I seem to be," she returned placidly. And Macartney gave me the despairing glance of a sensible man who had tried his best to head off a girl's silly whim, and failed.

"It's as you like," he said—to her, not to me. "But you understand you can't get back tonight, if you go to Caraquet. And—Good heavens—you ought *not* to go, if you want the truth of it! There's nothing to see—and you'll get half frozen—and you mayn't get back for days, if it snows!"

Paulette Brown looked at him as if he were not there. Then she laughed. "I didn't say I was going to Caraquet! If you want to know all about my taking a chance for a drive behind a pair of good horses, Miss Wilbraham wants Billy Jones's wife to come over for a week and work for her. I'm going to stay all night with Mrs. Jones and bring her back in the morning. She'll never leave Billy unless she's fetched. So I really think you needn't worry, Mr. Macartney," she paused, and I thought I saw him wince. "I'm not going to be a nuisance either to you or Mr. Stretton," and before he had a chance to answer she started up the horses. I had just time to take a flying jump and land in the wagon beside her as she drove off.

Macartney exclaimed sharply, and I didn't wonder. If he had not jumped clear the near wheels must have struck him. I lost the angry, startled sentence he snapped out. But it could have been nothing in particular, for my dream girl only turned in her seat and smiled at him.

I had no smile as I took the reins from her. I had wanted a chance to be alone with her, and I had it: but I knew better than to think she was going to Billy Jones's for the sake of a drive with me. The only real thought I had was that behind me, in the back of the wagon, were the boxes of gold she had marked inexplicably with her blue seal, and that I had heard her say the night before that she "would have to get that gold!"

How she meant to do it was beyond me; and it was folly to think she ever *could* do it, with six feet of a man's strength beside her. But nevertheless, when you loved a girl for no other earthly reason than that she was your dream of a girl come true, and even though she belonged to another man, it was no thought with which to start on a lonely drive with her. I set my teeth on it and never opened them for a solid mile over the hummocky road through the endless spruce bush, behind which the sun had already sunk. I could feel my dream girl's shoulder where she sat beside me, muffled in a sable-lined coat of Dudley's: and the sweet warmth of her, the faint scent of her gold-bronze hair, made me afraid to speak, even if I had known what I wanted to say.

But suddenly she spoke to me. "Mr. Stretton, you're not angry with me for coming with you?"

"You know I'm not." But I did not know what I was. Any one who has read as far as this will know that if ever a plain, stupid fool walked this world, it was I—Nicholas Dane Stretton. Put me in the bush, or with horses, and I'm useful enough—but with men and women I seem to go blind and dumb. I know I never could read a detective story; the clues and complications always made me feel dizzy. I was pretty well dazed where I sat beside that girl I knew I ought to find out about, and her nearness did not help me to ask her ugly questions. If she had not been Dudley's—but I broke the thought short off. I said to myself impersonally that it was impossible for a girl to do any monkey tricks about the La Chance gold with a man like me. Yet I wondered if she meant to try!

But she showed no sign of it. "I had to come," she said gently. "Marcia really wants Billy Jones's wife: she won't let me wait on her, and of course Charliet can't do it. You believe me, don't you? I didn't come just for a drive with you!"

I believed that well enough, and I nodded.

"Then," said my dream girl quietly, "will you please stop the horses?"

I looked round. We were miles from the mine, around a turn where the spruce bush ceased for a long stretch of swamp—bare, featureless, and frozen. Then, for the first time, I looked at Dudley's girl that I was fool enough to love.

"What for?" I demanded. "I mean, of course, if you like," for I saw she was white to the lips, though her eyes met mine steadily, like a man's. "Do you mean you want to go back?"

She shook her head almost absently. "No: I think there's something bumping around in the back of the wagon. I"—there was a sharp, nervous catch in her voice—"want to find out what it is."

I had packed the wagon, and I knew there was nothing in it to bump. But I stopped the horses. I wondered if the girl beside me had some sort of baby revolver and thought she could hold me up with it, if I let her get out; and I knew just what I would do if she tried it. I smiled as I waited. But she did not get out. She turned in her seat and reached backwards into the back of the wagon, as if she had neither bones nor joints in her lovely body. Marcia was right when she said it was perfectly educated and trained. For a moment I could think of nothing but the marvellous grace of her movement as she slid her hand under the tarpaulin that covered the gold; then I thought I heard her catch her breath with surprise. But she turned back with an exquisite lithe grace that made me catch mine, and slid down in her seat as if she had never slid out of it.

"It's a bottle," she said lightly. But it was with a kind of startled puzzle too, as if she had sooner expected dynamite. "I can't think why; I mean, I wonder what's in it!"

"A bottle!" I jerked around to stare at a whisky bottle in her hands. It was tightly sealed and full of something colorless that looked like gin. I was just going to say I could not see where it had come from, seeing I had packed the wagon myself, and I would have gone bail there was no bottle in it. But it came over me that she might be pretending astonishment and have put the thing there herself while I was in my room getting my revolver; since there had been no one else near my wagon but Macartney, and he could not have left the horses' heads. It flashed on me that the baby beside me, being used to Dudley, might have drugged a little gin, thinking I would take various drinks on the way; and I nearly laughed out. But I said: "Back there was no place for a bottle. It's a wonder it didn't smash on the first bump!"

"Yes," said Paulette slowly. "Only I wonder—I mean I can't see—" and she paused, staring at the bottle with a thoughtful sort of frown. "I believe I'll hold it on my lap."

I was looking at the bottle too, where she held it with both fur-gloved hands; and I forgot to wonder if she were lying about it or not. For the gloves she wore were Dudley Wilbraham's, as well as the coat—and that any of Dudley's things should be on my dream girl put me in a black, senseless fury. I wanted to take them straight off her and wrap her up in my own belongings. I grabbed at anything to say that would keep my tongue from telling her to change coats with me that instant, and the bottle in her hand was the only thing that occurred to me. It brought a sudden recollection back to me anyhow, and I opened my lips quite easily.

"Scott, that looks like some of the brew I spilled over my clothes at Skunk's Misery!"

"Skunk's Misery!" Paulette exclaimed sharply. "What on earth is Skunk's Misery?"

"A village—at least, a den—of dirt, chiefly; off this road, between Caraquet and Lac Tremblant." I was thankful to have something to think about that was neither her, or me, or Dudley. I made as long a story as I could of my stay in Skunk's Misery when I took home the half-killed boy; of the filthy stuff I had spilled on my clothes, and how I had seen a wolf carry them off. "By George, I believe he *liked* the smell—though I never thought of that till now!"

"What?" Paulette gave a curious start that might have been wonder, or enlightenment. "And you got the stuff at Skunk's Misery, out of a bottle like this? Oh, I ought to have guessed"—but she either checked herself, or her pause was absolutely natural—"I should have guessed you'd had some sort of a horrible time that night you came home. You looked so tired. But what I meant to say was I don't see how such poor people would have a bottle of *anything*. Didn't they say what it was?"

"Didn't ask! It looked like gin, and it smelt like a sulphide factory when it got on my clothes. They certainly had that bottle."

"Well, Skunk's Misery hasn't got *this* bottle, anyhow!" I could see no reason for the look on her face. It was not gay any more; it was stern, if a girl's face can be stern, and it was white with angry suspicion. Suddenly she laughed, rather fiercely. "I'm glad I thought of it before the jolting broke it in the wagon! I want to get it safely to Billy Jones's."

The reason why beat me, since she had pretended to know nothing of it, so I said nothing. After a long silence Paulette sighed.

"You've been very kind to me, Mr. Stretton," she said, as if she had been thinking. "I wish you could see your way to—trusting me!"

"I don't know how I've been kind," I left out the trusting part. "I have hardly seen you to speak to till tonight, except," and I said it deliberately, "the first time I ever saw you, sitting by the fire at La Chance. You did speak to me then."

"Was that—the first time you saw me?" It might have been forgetfulness, or a challenge to repeat what she had said to me by the lake in the dark. But I was not going to repeat that. Something told me, as it had told me when I came on her by Dudley's fire—though it was for a different reason, now that I knew she was his and not mine—that I would be a fool to fight my own thoughts of her with explanations, even if she chose to make any. I looked directly into her face instead. All I could see was her eyes, that were just dark pools in the dusk, and her mouth, oddly grave and unsmiling. But then and there—and anyone who thinks me a fool is welcome to—my ugly suspicions of her died. And I could have died of shame myself to think I had ever harbored them. If she had done things I could not understand—and she had—I knew there must be a good reason for them. For the rest, in spite of Marcia and her silly mysteries, and even though she belonged to Dudley, she was my dream girl, and I meant to stand by her.

"That was the first time I spoke to you," I said, as if there had been no pause. "After that, I picked up a seal for you, and I told you your hair was untidy before Marcia could. I think those are all the enormously kind things I've ever done for you. But, if you want kindness, you know where to come!"

"Without telling you things—and when you don't trust me!"

"Telling things never made a man trust anyone," said I. "And besides," it was so dark now, as we crawled along the side of the long rocky hill that followed the swamp, that I had to look hard to see her face, "I never said I didn't trust you. And there isn't anything you could tell me that I want to know!"

"Oh," Paulette cried as sharply as if I had struck her, "do you mean you're taking me on trust—in spite of everything?"

"In spite of nothing." I laughed. I was not going to have her think I knew about Collins, much more all the stuff Marcia had said. But she turned her head and looked at me with a curious intentness.

"I'll try," she began in a smothered sort of voice, "I mean I'm not all you've been thinking I was, Mr. Stretton! Only," passionately, and it was the last thing I had expected her to say, "I wish we were at Billy Jones's with all this gold!"

I did not, whether she had astonished me or not. I could have driven all night with her beside me, and her arm touching mine when the wagon bumped over the rocks.

"We're halfway," I returned rather cheerlessly. "Why? You're not afraid we'll be held up, are you? No human being ever uses this road."

"I wasn't thinking of human beings," she returned simply. "I was thinking of wolves."

"Wolves?" I honestly gasped it. Then I laughed straight out. "I can't feel particularly agitated about wolves. I know we had some at La Chance, but we probably left them there, nosing round the bunk-house rubbish heap. And anyhow, a wolf or two wouldn't trouble us. They're cowardly things, unless they're in packs." I felt exactly as if I were comforting Red Riding Hood or someone in a fairy tale, for the Lord knows it had never occurred to me to be afraid of wolves. "What on earth put wolves in your head?"

"I—don't know! They seemed to be about, lately."

"Well, I never saw any on this road! I've a revolver, anyhow."

"I'm g-glad," said Paulette; and the word jerked out of her, and my arms jerked nearly out of me. In the dark the wagon had hit something that felt like nothing but a boulder in the middle of my decent road. The wagon stopped dead, with an up-ending lurch, and nothing holding it to the horses but the reins. Why on earth they held I don't know. For with one almighty bound my two young horses tried to get away from me—and they would have, if the reins had not been new ones. As it was I had a minute's hard fighting before I got them under. When they stood still the girl beside me peered over the front of the wagon into the dark. "It's the whiffletree, I think," she said, as if she were used to wagons.

I peered over myself and hoped so. "Mercy if it is," said I. "If it's a wheel we're stuck here. Scott, I wonder if I've a bit of rope!"

Paulette Brown pulled out ten feet of spun yarn from under her coat; and if you come to think of it, it was a funny thing for a girl to have. It struck me, rather oddly, that she must have come prepared for accidents. "There," she said, "I expect you can patch us up if I hold the horses. Here's a knife, too, and"—I turned hot all over, for she was putting something else into my hand, just as if she knew I had been wondering about it since first we started; but she went on without a break—"here's my revolver. Put it in your pocket. I'd sooner you kept it."

I was thankful I had had the decency to trust her before she gave the weapon to me. But I was blazingly angry with myself when I got out of the wagon and saw just what had happened. Fair in the middle of my new road was a boulder that the frost must have loosened from the steep hillside that towered over us; and the front of the wagon had hit it square—which it would not have done if I had been looking at the road instead of talking to a girl who was no business of mine, now or ever. I got the horses out of the traces and the pole straps, and let Paulette hold them while I levered the boulder out of the way, down the hillside. I was scared to do it, too, for fear they would get away from her, but she was evidently as used to horses as to wagons: Bob and Danny stood for her like lambs, while I set to work to repair damages. The pole was snapped, and the whiffletree smashed, so that the traces were useless. I did some fair jury work with a lucky bit of spruce wood, the whiffletree, and the axle, and got the pole spliced. It struck me that even so we should have to do the rest of the way to Billy Jones's at a walk, but I saw no sense in saying so. I got the horses back on the pole, and Paulette in the wagon holding the reins, still talking to the horses quietly and by name. But as I jumped up beside her the quiet flew out of her voice.

"The *bottle*," she all but shrieked at me. "*Mind the bottle!*"

But I had not noticed she had put it on my seat when she got out to hold the horses. I knocked it flying across her, and it smashed to flinders on the near fore wheel, drenching it and splashing over Danny's hind legs. I grabbed the reins from Paulette, and I thought of skunks, and a sulphide factory—and dead skunks and rotten sulphide at that. Even in the freezing evening air the smell that came from that smashed bottle was beyond anything on earth or purgatory, excepting the stuff I had spilt over myself at Skunk's Misery. "What on earth," I began stupidly. "Why, that's that Skunk's Misery filth again!"

Paulette's hand came down on my arm with a grip that could not have been wilder if she had thought the awful smell meant our deaths. "Drive on, will you?" she said in a voice that matched it. "Let the horses *go*, I tell you! If there's anything left in that bottle it may save us for a—I mean," she caught herself up furiously, "it may save me from being sick. I don't know how you feel. But for heaven's sake get me out of that smell! Oh, why didn't I throw the thing away into the woods, long ago?"

I wished she had. The stuff was on Danny as well as on the wheel, and we smelt like a procession of dead whales. For after the first choking explosion of the thing it reeked of nothing but corruption. It was the Skunk's Misery brew all right, only a thousand times stronger.

"How on earth did Skunk's Misery filth get in my wagon?" I gasped. And if I had been alone I would have spat.

"I—can't tell you," said Paulette shortly. "Mr. Stretton, can't you hurry the horses? I— Oh, hurry them, please!"

I saw no particular reason why; we could not get away from the smell of the wheel, or of Danny. But I did wind them up as much as I dared with our kind of a pole—and suddenly both of them wound themselves up, with a jerk to try any pole. I had all I could do to keep them from a dead run, and if I knew the reason I trusted the girl beside me did not. It had hardly been a sound, more the ghost of a sound. But as I thought it she flung up her head.

"What's that?" she said sharply. "Mr. Stretton, what's that?"

"Nothing," I began; and changed it. "Just a wolf or two somewhere."

For behind us, in two, three, four quarters at once rose a long wailing howl.

# CHAPTER 6

## MOSTLY WOLVES: AND A GIRL

*Oh, what was that drew screaming breath?*
*"A wolf that slashed at me!"*
*Oh, who was that cried out in death?*
*"A man who struck at thee!"*
　　　　　　　—The Night Ride.

The sound might have come from a country hound or two baying for sheer melancholy, or after a cat: only there were neither hounds nor cats on the Caraquet road. I felt Paulette stiffen through all her supple body. She whispered to herself sharply, as if she were swearing—only afterwards I knew better, and put the word she used where it belonged: "The devil! Oh, the devil!"

I made no answer. I had enough business holding in the horses, remembering that spliced pole. Paulette remembered it too, for she spoke abruptly. "How fast do you dare go?"

"Oh, not too fast," my thoughts were still on the pole. "They're not after us, if you're worrying about those wolves."

But she took no notice. "How far are we from Billy Jones's?"

We were a good way. But I said, "Oh, a few miles!"

"Well, we've got to make it!" I could still feel her strangely rigid against my arm; perhaps it was only because she was listening. But—quick, like life, or death, or anything else sudden as lightning—she had no need to listen; nor had I. A burst of ravening yells, gathering up from all sides of us except in front, came from the dark bush. And I yelled myself, at Bob and Danny, to keep them off the dead run.

It was rot, of course, but I had a uncanny feeling that wolves *were* after us, and that it was just that Skunk's Misery stuff that had started them, as it had drawn the wolf that had taken my clothes. I could hear the yelping of one after another grow into the full-throated chorus of a pack. The woods were full of them.

"I didn't think he'd dare," Paulette exclaimed, as if she came out of her secret thoughts.

But it did not bring me out of mine, even to remember that young devil Collins. I had pulled out my gun to scare the wolves with a shot or two—and there were no cartridges in it! I could not honestly visualize myself filling it up the night before, but I was sure I had filled it, just as I was sure I had never troubled to look at it since. But of course I could not have, or it would not have been empty now. I inquired absently, because I was rummaging my pockets for cartridges, "Who'd dare? *Whoa*, Bob! What he?"

"They," Paulette corrected sharply. "I meant the wolves. I thought they were cowards, but—they don't sound cowardly! I—Mr. Stretton, I believe I'm worried!"

So was I, with a girl to take care of, a tied-on pole and whiffletree, and practically no gun; for there was not a single loose cartridge in my pockets. I had been so mighty secure about the Caraquet road I had never thought of them. I cursed inside while I said disjointedly, "Quiet, Bob, will you?— There's nothing to be afraid of; you'll laugh over this tonight!" Because I suddenly hoped so—if the pole held to the Halfway—for the infernal clamor behind us had dropped abruptly to what might have been a distant dog fight. But at a sudden note in it the sweat jumped to my upper lip.

"Dunn and Collins!" I thought. They had been missing when we left. Paulette had said she did not trust Collins, and since he had had the *nous* to get hold of the Skunk's Misery wolf dope, he or Dunn could easily have stowed it in my wagon in the night, and been caught by it themselves where they had started out to waylay us by the boulder they put in my road. But all I said was, "The wolves have stopped!"

"Not they," Paulette retorted, and suddenly knocked me silly with surprise. "Oh, I haven't done you a bit of good by coming, Mr. Stretton! I thought if I were with you I might be some use, and I'm not."

I stared stupidly. "D'ye mean you came to fight wolves?"

"No! I came—" but she stopped. "I was afraid—I mean I hated your going alone with all that gold, and Marcia really wanted Mrs. Jones."

Any other time I would have rounded on her and found out what she was keeping back, but I was too busy thinking. The horses had calmed to a flying trot up the long hill along whose side we had been crawling when the pole went. Once over the crest of it we should have done two miles since we heard the first wolf howl; which meant we were nearer to Billy Jones's than I had remembered. If the pole held to get us down the other side of the long hill there was nothing before us but a mile of corduroy road through a jungle-thick swamp of hemlock, and then the one bit of really excellent going my road could boast—three clear miles, level as a die, straight to the Halfway stables.

"We haven't far now," said I shortly. "And it doesn't matter why you came; you've been useful enough! I couldn't have held the horses and patched the wagon too." I omitted to say I could have tied them to a wheel. "But if you're nervous now, there's one thing we could do. Can you ride?"

"*Ride?*" I thought she laughed. "Yes! Why?"

"We could cut the horses loose and ride them in to the Halfway."

"What? And leave the gold out here, as we were m—" I knew she cut off 'meant to.' "I won't do it!"

"Wolves wouldn't eat it—and there's no one to steal it," I returned matter-of-factly—because if Collins had meant to, the sinister flurry behind us had decided me his career was closed. "However, it would be wasting trouble to leave the stuff; there's no sign of any pack after us now." And a ravening yell cut the words off my tongue.

The brutes must have scoured after us in silence, hunting us in the dark for the last mile. For as we stood out, a black blot on the hilltop against the night sky, they broke out in chorus just behind us, for all the world like a pack of hounds who had treed a wildcat; and too close for any fool lying to occur to me.

"Paulette," I blurted, "there's not a cartridge in my gun! Yours is so little I'm afraid of it. But it may scare them. Take these reins!"

But she turned in her seat and knelt there, looking behind us. If I could have got her on Danny's back and let her run clear five minutes ago it was impossible now. No human being could have pulled up Bob or him.

"See them?" I snapped. "By heaven, I wish the brutes would stop that yelling; they're driving the horses crazy! See them?"

"No. But—yes, yes," her voice flashed out sharp as a knife. "They're on us! Give me the revolver, quick! I can shoot; and I've cartridges. You couldn't do any good with it: it throws low—and it's too small for your hand. And I wouldn't dare drive. I might get off the road, and we'd be done."

It was so true that I did not even turn my head as I shoved over her little gun. I had no particular faith in her shooting; my trust was in the horses' speed. We were getting down the hill like a Niagara of galloping hoofs and wheels over a road I had all I could do to see; with that crazy pole I dared not check the horses to put an ounce on. I stood up and drove for all I was worth, and the girl beside me shot—and hit! For a yell and a screaming flurry rose with every report of her revolver. It was a beastly noise, but it rejoiced me; till suddenly I heard her pant out a sickened sentence that made me gasp, because it was such a funny thing to say.

"My heavens, I never thought I could be cruel to animals—like this. But I've got to do it. I"— her voice rose in sudden disjointed triumph—"Mr. Stretton, I believe I've stopped them!"

"I believe you have," I swore blankly—and one leapt out of the dark by the fore wheel as I spoke, and she shot it.

But it was the last; she *had* stopped them. And if I had not known that to have turned even one eye from my horses as we tore down that hill would have meant we were smashed up on one side of it, I would have been more ashamed than I was of being fought for by a girl. "You're a wonder—just a marvellous wonder," I got out thickly. "We're clear—and it's thanks to you!" And ahead of us, in the jungle-thick hemlock that crowded the sides of the narrow road I had corduroyed through the swamp for a ricketty mile, a single wolf howled.

It had a different, curious note, a dying note, if I had known it; but I did not realize it then. I thought, "We're done! They've headed us!" I said, "Look out ahead for all you're worth. If we can keep going, we'll be through this thicket in a minute."

But Paulette cut out my thought. "We *are* done, if they throw the horses!" And instantly, amazingly, she stood up in the bumping, swaying wagon as if she were on a dancing floor and shed Dudley Wilbraham's coat. She leaned toward me, and I felt rather than saw that she was in shirt and knickerbockers like a boy. "Keep the horses going as steady as you can, and whatever you do, don't try to stop them. I'm going to do something. Mind, keep them *galloping!*"

I would have grabbed her; only before I knew what she was going to do she was past me, out over the dashboard, and running along the smashed pole between Bob and Danny in the dark.

It was nothing to do in daylight. I've done it myself before now, and so have most men. But for a girl, in the dark and on a broken pole, with wolves heading the horses—I was so furiously afraid for her that the blood stopped running in my legs, and it was a minute before I saw what she was after. She had not slipped; she was astride Danny—ducking under his rein neatly, for I had not felt the sign of a jerk—but only God knew what might happen to her if he fell. And suddenly I knew what she had run out there to do. She was shooting ahead of the horses, down the road; then to one side and the other of it impartially, covering them. Only what knocked me was that there was no sign of a wolf either before or beside us on the narrow, black-dark highway—and that she was shooting into the jungle-thick swamp hemlocks on each side of it at the breast height of a man!

And at a single ghastly, smothered cry I burst out, "By gad, it *is* men!" For I knew she had shot one. I listened, over the rattling roll of the wheels on the corduroy, but there was no second cry. There was only what seemed dead silence after the thunder of the wheels on the uneven logs, as we swept out on the level road that led straight to the Halfway stable. It was light, too, after the dead blackness of the narrow swamp road. I saw the girl turn on Danny carelessly, as if she were in a saddle, and wave her hand forward for me to keep going. But the only thought I had was to get her back into the wagon. Not because I was afraid of a smash, for if the mended pole had held in that crazy, tearing gallop from the top of the hill it would hold till the Halfway. I just wanted her safe beside me. I had had enough of seeing a girl do stunts that stopped my blood. "Come back out of that," I shouted at her; "I'm going to stop the horses—and you come *here*!"

She motioned forward, crying out something unintelligible. But before I could pull up the horses, before I even guessed what she meant to do, I saw her stand up on Danny's back, spring from his rump, and—land lightly in the wagon!

It may be true that I damned her up in heaps from sheer fright; I know I asked fiercely if she wanted to kill herself. She said no, quite coolly. Only that that pole would not bear any more running on it, or the jerk of a sudden stop either: it was that she had called out to me.

"Neither can I bear any more—of tricks that might lose your life to save me and my miserable gold," I said angrily. "Sit down this minute and wrap that coat round you." I had ceased to care that it was Dudley's. "It's bitter cold. And there's the light at the Halfway!"

"What I did wasn't anything—for me," my dream girl retorted oddly. "And I don't know that it was altogether to save you, Mr. Stretton, or your gold either, that you thought I meant to steal. I was pretty afraid for myself, with those wolves!"

I was too raging with myself to answer. Of course it had not been she who had meant to steal my gold; and no matter how she had known someone meant to get at me, with wolves or anything else. It had been just Collins— and the sheer gall of it jammed my teeth—Collins and Dunn, two ne'er-do-well brats in our own mine. I had realized already that they had been missing from La Chance quite early enough for me to thank them for the boulder on my good road, and Collins— But I hastily revised my conviction that it was Collins I had heard the wolves chop in the bush as hounds chop a fox: Collins had too much sense. It had more likely been Dunn; he was the kind to get eaten! Collins must have legged it early for my corduroy road, where Paulette had expected him enough to shoot at him; while Dunn stayed round La Chance to put the wolf bait in my wagon and got caught by it himself on his way to join Collins.

As for the genesis of the wolf dope, its history came to me coherently as letters spelling a word, beginning with the bottle of mixed filth I had spilt on myself at Skunk's Misery. The second I and my smelly clothes reached shore the night I returned to La Chance, a wolf had scented me and howled; had followed me to the shack and howled again while I was talking to Marcia about Paulette Brown; and another had carried off those very clothes under my own eyes where I stood by my window, as if the smell on them had been some kind of bait it could not resist. Wherever Dunn and Collins had got it, the smell from the broken bottle had been exactly the same, only twenty times stronger: and it had been meant to smash at the boulder on my road and turn me into a living bait for wolves!

The theory may sound crazy, but it happens to be sane. There is a wolf dope, made of heaven knows what, except that it contains certain ingredients that have to be put in bottles and ripened in the sun for a month. Two Frenchmen were jailed this last June in Quebec province for using it around a fish and game club, and endangering people's lives. That same wolf bait had been put in my wagon by somebody—and the human cry out of the swamp at Paulette's shot suddenly repeated itself in my ears. I was biting my lip, or I would have grinned. Paulette had hit the man who was to have put me out of business, if the wolves failed when that bottle smashed and the boulder crippled my wagon. Collins, who, laid up in the swamp, was to have reaped my gold and me if I got through! The cheek of him made me blaze again, and I turned on Paulette abruptly.

"Look here, do you know you shot a man in the swamp?"

"I hope I killed him," returned that same girl who had disliked being cruel to wolves—and instantly saw what I was after. "That's nonsense, though! There couldn't have been any man there, Mr. Stretton. The wolves would have eaten him!"

"Only one wolf got by you," I suggested drily.

She shrugged her shoulders. "They'd have shot at us—men, I mean!"

I made no answer. It struck me forcibly that Collins certainly would have; unless he was not out for shooting, but merely waiting to remove the gold from my wagon as soon as the wolves had disposed of my horses and me. Even then I did not see why he had held his fire, unless he had no gun. But the whole thing was a snarl it was no good thinking about till the girl beside me owned how much she knew about it. I wondered sharply if it had been just that knowledge she was trying to give Dudley the night I stopped her. The lights at the Halfway were very close as I turned to her.

"If I've helped you at all, why can't you tell me all the trouble, instead of Dudley?" I asked, very low.

"I don't know anything," but I thought she checked a sob, "that I—can tell. I just thought there might be trouble tonight, but I imagined it would happen before you started. That was why I marked that gold. Don't take any, *ever*, out of the safe, if it hasn't my seal on it."

"You can't prevent Collins from changing the boxes—forever," I said deliberately; because, unless he were dead, as I hoped, she couldn't. But Paulette stared at me, open-lipped, as we drove into the Halfway yard, and Billy Jones ran out with a lantern.

"Collins?" she repeated, as if she had never heard his name, much less met him secretly in the dark. "I don't know anything about any Collins, nor anyone I could—put a name to! I tell you I don't know who was in the swamp!"

She had not said she did not know who was responsible for the bottle in my wagon. But if I am Indian-dark I can be Indian-silent too. I said nothing about that. "Well, it doesn't matter who did anything," I exclaimed suddenly, "so long as there's trust between you and me!" Because I forgot Dudley and everything but my dream girl who had fought for me, and I suddenly wondered if she had not forgotten Dudley, too. For Bob and Danny stood still, played out and sweating, and Paulette Brown sat staring at me with great eyes, instead of moving.

But she had forgotten nothing. "You're very kind—to me, and Dudley," she said quietly, and slipped out of the wagon before I could lift her down. A sudden voice kept me from jumping after her.

"By golly," said Billy Jones, sniffing at my fore wheel. "Have you run over a hundred skunks?"

# CHAPTER 7

## I FIND LITTLE ENOUGH ON THE CORDUROY ROAD, AND LESS AT SKUNK'S MISERY

I told Billy Jones as much as I thought fit of the evening's work—which included no mention of wolf dope, or shooting on the corduroy road.

If he listened incredulously to my tale of a wolf pack one look at Bob and Danny told him it was true. They had had all they wanted, and we spent an hour working over them. The wagon was a wreck; why the spliced pole had hung together to the Halfway I don't know, but it had; and I let the smell on it go as a skunk. I lifted the gold into the locked cupboard where Billy kept his stores. It had to be put in another wagon for Caraquet, anyhow; and besides, I was not going on to Caraquet in the morning. The gold was safe with Billy, and there were other places that needed visiting first. There was no hope of getting at the ugly business that had brewed up at La Chance through Paulette Brown, or Collins either; since one would never tell how much or how little she knew, and the other would lie, if he ever reappeared. But the wolf bait end I could get at, and I meant to. Which was the reason I sat on one of the horses I had sent over to the Halfway—after my one experience when it held none—when my dream girl and Mrs. Jones came out of Billy's shack in the cold of a November dawn.

"I'm riding some of the way back with you," I observed casually.

Paulette stopped short. She was lovelier than I had ever seen her, with her gold-bronze hair shining over the sable collar of Dudley's coat. I fancied her eyes shone, too, for one second, at seeing me. But there I was wrong.

"I thought you'd started for Caraquet," she exclaimed hastily. "You needn't come with us. There won't be any wolves in the daytime, and—you know there's no need for you to come!"

There was not. Even if her voice had not so significantly conveyed the fact that there was no bottle in her wagon this time, Mrs. Billy Jones—to put a hard fact politely—was about the most capable lady I had ever met. She was big-boned, hard-faced and profane; and usually left Billy to look after the house while she attended to a line of traps, or hunted bears for their skins.

No wolves would worry the intrepid and thoroughly armed Mrs. Jones. But all the same I was riding some of the way back to La Chance.

There was not a thing to be seen on the corduroy road through the swamp, or on the hill we had come down at the dead run; and I had not expected there would be. But on the top of the hill I bade good-bye to my dream girl—who was not mine and was going back to Dudley. It was all I could manage to do it, too. I did not know I was biting my lip until it hurt; then I stopped watching her out of sight and turned back on the business that had brought me.

You could ride a horse down the hill into the swamp if you knew how; and I did. I tied him to a tree and went over each side of the corduroy road on my feet. It was silent as death there in the cold gray morning, with the frost-fog clinging in the somber hemlocks, and the swamp frozen so solid that my moccasins never left a mark. No one else's feet had left a mark there, either, and I would have given up the idea that a man had been cached by the road the night before, if it had not been for two things.

One was a dead wolf, with a gash in his throat in which the knife had been left till he was cold; you could tell by the blood clots round the wound: the other I did not find at once. But wolves do not stab themselves, and I remembered that the lone wolf cry ahead of us on that road had been a dying cry, not a hunting one. If Collins had killed the beast he had waited there long enough to let an hour pass before he took his knife out of its throat: so he had been there when we raced by—which was all I wanted to know, except where he had gone since. As for the other thing I found, it was behind the hemlocks when I quartered the sides of the road in the silence and the frost-fog: and it was nothing but a patch of shell ice. But the flimsy, crackling stuff was crushed into two cup-like marks, as plainly telltale as if I had seen a man fall on his knees in them. And by them, frozen there, were a dozen drops of blood.

I knew angrily that if it were Collins's blood he had not missed it particularly, for he had moved away without leaving a sign of a trail. Where to I had no means of knowing, till five minutes later I found another spatter of blood on my corduroy road—and as I looked at it my own blood boiled. There was not only no one but that young devil Collins who could have lain in wait for me; but he had had the nerve to walk away on my own road! Where to, beat me; but considering what I knew of his easy deviltry it was probably back to La Chance and a girl who was daring to fight him,

If I were worried for that girl I could not go back to her. I had to get my gold to Caraquet. Besides, I had a feeling it might be useful to do a little still hunting round Skunk's Misery. If Collins had had that bottle of devil's brew at La Chance he had got it from Skunk's Misery: probably out of the very hut where I had once nursed a filthy boy. And I had a feeling that the first thing I needed to do was to prove it.

As I rode back to Billy Jones's I would have given a deal for any kind of a motor car that would have reduced the twenty-seven miles to Caraquet into nothing, instead of an all-day job—which it proved to be.

Not that I met a soul on the road. I didn't. But it took my wagon four hours to reach Caraquet over the frozen ruts of that same road; and another hour to hand over Dudley's gold to Randall, a man of my own who was to carry it on the mail coach to the distant railway.

I had no worry about the gold, once Randall had charge of it: no one was likely to trouble him or the coach on the open post road, even if they had guessed what he convoyed. I was turning away, whistling at being rid of the stuff, when he called me back to hand over a bundle of letters for La Chance. There were three for Marcia, and one—in old Thompson's back-number copperplate—for Dudley. There were no letters for Paulette Brown or myself, but perhaps neither of us had expected any. I know I hadn't. I gave the Wilbraham family's correspondence the careless glance you always bestow on other people's letters and shoved it into my inside pocket. After which I left my horses and wagon safe in Randall's stable and started to walk back to Skunk's Misery and the Halfway stables.

It seemed a fool thing to do, and I had no particular use for walking all that way; but there was no other means of accomplishing the twenty miles through the bush from Caraquet to Skunk's Misery. Aside from the fact that I had no desire to advertise my arrival, there was no wagon road to Skunk's Misery. Its inhabitants did not possess wagons—or horses to put in them.

It was black dark when I reached the place, and for a moment I stood and considered it. I had never really visualized it before, any more than you do any place that you take for granted as outside your scheme of existence. I was not so sure that it was, now. Anyhow, I stood in the gap of a desolate hill and looked into the hollow before me that—added to the dirt no skunk could stand—had earned the place its name. It was all stones: gravel stones, little stones, stones as big as cabs and as big as houses; and, hunched up among them like lean-tos, hidden away among the rocks and the pine trees grow-ing up from among the rocks wherever they could find root-hold, were the houses of the Skunk's Misery people. There was no pretense of a street or a village: there were just houses—if they deserved even that name. How many there were I could not tell. I had never had the curiosity to explore the place. But if it sounds as though a narrow, stone-choked valley were no citadel for a man or men to have hidden themselves, or for anyone to conduct an industry like making a secret scent to attract wolves, the person who said so would be mistaken. There was never in the world a better place for secret dwelling and villainy and all the rest than Skunk's Misery.

In the first place, you could not see the houses among the rocks. The valley was just like a porcupine warren. No rock stood out alone: they were all jumbled up together, big and little, with pine trees growing on the tops of them and in between them, up from the earth that was twelve, twenty, or sometimes forty feet below. The whole hollow was a maze of narrow, winding tracks, between rocks and under them, sometimes a foot wide and sometimes six, that Skunk's Misery used for roads. What its citizens lived on, I had never been able to guess. Caraquet said it was on wolf bounties—which was another thing that had set me thinking about the bottle I had spilt on my clothes. If Collins or Dunn had got a similar bottle there I meant to find out about it: and I had the more heart for doing it since Paulette Brown knew nothing of Skunk's Misery. You can tell when a girl has never heard of a place, and I knew she had never heard of that one. I settled down the revolver I had filled up at Billy Jones's, and trod softly down the nearest of the winding alleys, over the worn pine needles, in the dark.

There were just twenty houses, when I had counted all I could find. There might have been twenty more, under rocks and behind rocks I could not make my way around; but I was no porcupine, and in the dark I could not stumble on them. There was not a sign of a stranger in the place, or a soul about. And judging from the darkness and the quiet, all the fat-faced, indifferent women were in bed and asleep, and the shiftless rats of men were still away. There were no dogs to bark at me: I had learned that in my previous sojourn there. Dogs required food, and Skunk's Misery had none to spare. I went back through the one winding alley that was familiar to me, found the hut where I had nursed the boy, and walked in.

There was not any Collins there, anyhow. The boy and his mother were in bed, or what went for being in bed. But at the sound of my voice the woman fairly flung herself at me, saying that her son was recovered again, and it was I who had saved him for her. She piled wood on the fire that was built up against the face of the rock that formed two sides of her house, and jabbered gratitude as I had never thought any Skunk's Misery woman could jabber. And she did not look like one, either; she was handsome, in a haggard, vicious way, and she was not old. I did not think myself that her son looked particularly recovered. He lay like a log on his spruce-bough bed, awake and conscious but wholly speechless, though his mother seemed satisfied. But I had not come to talk about any sick boys. I asked casually where I could find the stranger who had been in Skunk's Misery lately. But the woman only stared at me, as if the idea would not filter into her head. Presently she said dully that there had been no stranger there; I was the only one she had ever seen.

It was likely enough; a Skunk's Misery messenger had more probably taken the wolf dope to Collins. I asked casually if she had any more of the stuff I had spilt on my clothes, and where she had got it—and once more I ran bang up against a stone wall. The woman explained matter-of-factly that she had not got it from anyone. She had found it standing in the sun beside one of the rocks, and stolen it, supposing it was gin. When she found it was not she took it for some sort of liniment; and put it where I had knocked it over on myself. She had never seen nor heard of any more of it. But of course it might have belonged to anyone in the place, only I could understand she could not ask about it: which I did, knowing how precious a whole bottle of anything was in those surroundings. As to where she had found it, she could not be sure. She thought it was by the new house the Frenchwoman's son had built that autumn and never lived in!

I pricked up my ears. The Frenchwoman's son was one of the men arrested in Quebec province for using wolf dope: a handsome, elusive devil who sometimes haunted the lumber woods at the lower end of Lac Tremblant, trapping or robbing traps as seemed good to him, and paying back interruptions with such interest that no one was keen to interfere with him. If the Frenchwoman's son were in with Collins in trying to hold up the La Chance gold and was at Skunk's Misery now, I saw daylight—anyhow about the wolf dope.

But the woman by the fire knocked that idea out of me, half-made. The Frenchwoman's son had not been there for two months past and had only come there at all to build a house. It was empty now, but no one had dared to go into it. She could show it to me, but she was sure he had had nothing to do with that liniment, if I wanted any more. After which she relapsed into indifference, or I thought so, till I showed her what little money I had in my pocket. She rose then, abruptly, and led the way out of her hut to the deserted house the Frenchwoman's son had built for caprice and never lived in.

It was deserted enough, in all conscience. The door was open, and the November wind free to play through the place as it liked. I stood on the threshold, thinking. I had found out nothing about any wolf-bait, excepting the one bottle the Frenchwoman's son might or might not have left there; certainly nothing about Collins ever having got hold of any; and if I had meant to spend the rest of the night in Skunk's Misery I saw no particular sense in doing it. I had a solid conviction that the boy's mother would not mention I had ever been there, for fear she might have to share what little I had given her—which, as it fell out, was true—and turned to go.

But when the woman had left me to creep home in the dark, while I made my own way out of the village, I altered my mind about going. I cut down enough pine boughs to make a bed under me, shut the door of the deserted house—that I knew enough of the Frenchwoman's son to know would have no visitors—had a drink from my flask, and slept the sleep of the hunting dog till it should be daylight.

And, like the hunting dog, I went on with my business in my dreams; till my legs jerked and woke me, to see a waning moon peering in from the west, through the hole that served the hut for a chimney, and I rose to go back to Billy Jones. For I dreamed there was a gang of men in a cellar under the very hut I slept in, with a business-like row of wolf-bait bottles at their feet, where they sat squabbling over a poker game. But as I said, it was the waning morning moon that woke me, and the hut was silent as the grave. I picked up the pine-bough bed I had slept on and carried it into the bush with me far enough to throw it down where it would tell no tales—I did not know why I did it, but I was to be glad—tightened up my belt, and took a short cut through the thick bush to Billy Jones's stables, with nothing to show for my day's and night's work but a dead wolf, a stained bit of shell ice, and a few drops of blood on the logs of my corduroy road. I was starving, and it was noonday, when I came out of the bush and tramped into the Halfway, much as I had done that first time I came from Skunk's Misery and went home to La Chance. Only today Billy Jones was not sitting by his stove reading his ancient newspaper. He was standing in the kitchen with two teamsters from La Chance, looking down at a dead man.

As I opened the door and stood staring, the teamsters jumped as if they had been shot. But Billy only turned a stolid white face on me.

"My God, Mr. Stretton," he said, stolidly too, "what do you make of this?"

All I could see from where I stood was a rigid hand, that had said death to me the second I opened the door. I gave a sort of spring forward. What I thought was that here was the man who had left the blood in the swamp when Paulette's bullet hit him, and that I had got Collins. I had nearly burst out that he had what he deserved. But instead I stopped, paralyzed, where my spring had left me.

"My God," I said in my turn, "I don't know!"

For the man who lay in front of me, stone dead in water-soaked clothes that were frozen to his stark body, was Thompson, our old superintendent, who only six weeks ago had left the La Chance mine; whose letter to Dudley, with its careful, back-number copperplate address, lay in my pocket now.

"It's Thompson!" was the only thing I could say.

# CHAPTER 8

## THOMPSON!

Thompson it was, if it seemed incredible. And Billy Jones exclaimed, as he pointed to him, "He can't have been dead longer than since last night! And I can't understand this thing, Mr. Stretton! It's but six weeks since Thompson *left* here; and from what he said he didn't mean to come back. He told me he was in a hurry to get away, because he was taking a position in a copper mine in the West. I remember I warned him you hadn't got all your swamps corduroyed, and likely he couldn't drive clear into Caraquet; so he left his wagon here and borrowed a saddle from me to ride over. And a boy brought his horse back next day, or day after—I forget which. I remember Thompson forgot to send me a tin of tobacco he promised to get me off Randall, at Caraquet!"

"D'ye mean you think he never went to Caraquet?" It was a stupid question, for, of course, I knew he had gone there, and farther, or he could not have sent Macartney to La Chance, or a letter to Dudley now. But what I was really thinking of was that I had been right about the date old Thompson left the mine, and that he had gone over my road on one of the two days I was away with all my road men, getting logs out of the bush.

Billy Jones scattered my thoughts impatiently: "Oh, he went there all right. It's his—coming back—that beats me!"

It beat me too, for reasons Billy knew nothing about. Why Thompson had come back was his own business; but it was plain he had been dead a scant twenty-four hours, and the only place I could think of where he was likely to have been killed was on my corduroy road the night before. Only I did not see how Thompson's clothes could have got water-soaked in a frozen swamp; and I did not see, either, what a decent man like Thompson could have been doing out there like a wolf, with wolves. I had more sense than to think he could have had any truck with Collins about our gold. I nodded back at the teamsters: "Where did they find him?"

"They didn't find him," returned Billy simply, "it was my hound dog. He was yelling down at the lake shore this morning, like he'd treed a wildcat, and when I went down it was Thompson he'd found—lying right on shore in the daylight! You know how that fool Lac Tremblant behaves; the water in it had gone down to nothing this morning, and on the bare stones it had left was Thompson. Only I don't see how he ever *got* there unless he was coming back, from wherever he'd been outside, by Lac Tremblant instead of your road!"

"Where was his canoe?"

"He didn't have any! But you know that lake—it might have smashed his canoe on him like an egg, and then—just by chance—put him ashore!" I did know: I had had all I wanted to keep from being smashed myself the night I crossed to La Chance. I nodded, and Billy choked. "It—it kind of sickened me this morning; I *liked* Thompson, Mr. Stretton!"

So had I, if I had laughed at his eternal solitaire. Billy and I laid him on the bed, decently, after we had done what we could for him. And I was ashamed to have even wondered if he had been the man Paulette had shot at on the La Chance road; for there was not a mark on him, and a fool could have told he had just been drowned in Lac Tremblant. There was nothing in his pockets to tell how he had got there: only a single two-dollar bill and a damp pack of cards in a wet leather case. Thompson's solitaire cards! Somehow the things gave me a lump in my throat; I wished I had talked more to Thompson in the long evenings. The letter in my pocket from him was Dudley's, and I did not mention it to Billy. I said I would try to find out where the dead man had come from, and anything else I could, before he buried him. And with that I left old Thompson lying on Billy's bed with his face covered, and rode home to La Chance.

When I got in, Dudley and Macartney were in the living room, talking. Any other time I might have wondered why Dudley looked so jumpy and bad-tempered, but all I was thinking of then was my ugly news. But before I could tell it, Dudley flew at me. "Where the devil have you been all day? And what's happened to my gold?"

I don't know why, but I had a furious, cold qualm that either Dudley or Macartney had *found out*—I don't mean about Collins so much as about Paulette having been mixed up with him. Till I knew I was damned if I'd mention him.

"I don't understand," I said shortly. "The gold's in Caraquet. But the reason I didn't get home this morning is that Thompson's back!"

"What?" Macartney never spoke loud, yet it cracked out.

I nodded. "I mean he's dead, poor chap! They found his body in Lac Tremblant this morning." And suddenly I knew I was staring at Macartney. His capable face was always pale, but in one second it had gone ghastly. It came over me that he had known old Thompson all his life, and I blurted involuntarily, "I'm sorry, Macartney!"

But he took no notice.

"They found Thompson's body," he said heavily, as a man does when he is sick with shock. "Who found it? Why—he wasn't *here*! What in hell do you mean?"

I told him. Dudley sat and goggled at the two of us, but Macartney stared at the floor, his face still ghastly. "I beg your pardon, Stretton," he muttered as if he were dizzy. "Only Thompson was about the oldest friend I had. I thought—" But he checked himself and exclaimed with a sudden sharp doubt, "It can't be old Thompson, Stretton; you must be mistaken! He couldn't be here—he was going out West. I was expecting a letter from him any day, to say he'd started."

"It's here. At least, I mean there's *a* letter from him, that I got in Cara-quet, only it's for Mr. Wilbraham. And I wasn't mistaken, Macartney. I wish I were!"

Macartney could not speak. I was surprised; I had not suspected him of much of a heart. I pulled out the letter, and Dudley opened it.

"Down and out—the poor old devil," said he slowly, staring at it, "and came back. Well, poor Thompson!" He read the thing again and handed it to Macartney. But Macartney only gave one silent, comprehensive stare at it, in the set-eyed way that was the only thing I had never liked about him, and pushed the letter across the table to me.

It was dated and postmarked Montreal. There was no street address, which was not like Thompson. But its precise phrases, which *were* like him, sounded down and out all right.

"Dear Mr. Wilbraham:
"I write to inquire if you will take me back at La Chance. There is no work here, or anywhere, and the British Columbia copper mine, where I intended to go, has shut down. I have nothing else in view, and I am stranded. If by tomorrow I cannot obtain work here I see nothing between me and starvation but to return to La Chance. I trust you can see your way to taking me back, in no matter how subordinate a position, at least till I can hear of something else. If I am obliged to chance coming to you I will take the shortest route, avoiding Caraquet, and coming by Lac Tremblant.
"Yours truly,
"WILLIAM D. THOMPSON."

"That's funny," I let out involuntarily. And Dudley snapped at me that it wasn't; it was ghastly.

"I don't mean the letter," I said absently. "It's that about Lac Tremblant. Thompson was scared blue of that lake; he used to beg me not to go out on it. And by gad, Dudley, I don't see how he could have come that way! He couldn't paddle a canoe!"

"What?" Macartney started, staring at me. "You're right: he couldn't," he said slowly. "That does make it peculiar—except that we don't know he meant to paddle up the lake. He might have intended to walk here along its shore, and strayed or slipped in or something, in the dark. But what troubles me is—can't you see he'd gone crazy? This letter"—he put a finger on it, eloquently—"isn't sane, from a self-contained man like Thompson! He must have been off his head with worry before he wrote it, or started back to a place he'd left for—"

"Incompetency, if you want the brutal truth," Dudley broke in not unkindly. "He was too old-fashioned to make good elsewhere, I expect; and if he found it out, I don't wonder if he did go off his head."

I glanced over Dudley's shoulder at the letter he and Macartney were studying. It did not look crazy, with its Gaskell's Compendium copperplate and its careful signature. I don't know why I picked up the envelope from where it lay unnoticed on the table by Dudley and fiddled with it scrutinizingly, but I did. The outside of it looked all right, with its address in Thompson's neat copperplate. But it wasn't well glued or something, for as I shoved my fingers inside, the whole thing opened out flat, like a lily. I looked down mechanically as I felt it go, and—by gad, the inside of it *didn't* look right! There was nothing on the glued-down top flap, but the inside back of the envelope wasn't blank, as it should have been. It wasn't written on in Thompson's neat copperplate or in his neat phrases, either. A pencil scrawl stared at me, upside down, as I gripped the lower flap of the envelope unconsciously, under the ball of my big thumb. "Why, here's some more," I exclaimed like an ass, glaring at the envelope's inside back. "'Take care—something—' What's this? What on earth did the old man mean?"

Macartney caught the splayed-out envelope from my hand, so sharply that the flap I didn't know I held tore away, and stayed in my fist as he gazed on the rest of the reversed envelope with his set-eyed stare. "'Take care, Macartney! Gold, life, everything—in danger!'" he read out blankly. "Why, it's some kind of a crazy warning to *me*! Only—nobody wants my life, and I've no gold—if that's what he means! I—" but he broke down completely. "Old Thompson must have gone stark mad," he muttered. "I—it makes me heartsick!"

"I don't know," Dudley snapped unexpectedly. "It fits about the gold, perhaps. Thompson might have suspected something before he left here!"

He looked at Macartney significantly, and I remembered the question he had rapped at me when I came in. Something inside me told me to hold my tongue concerning my adventures on the Caraquet road till I knew what Paulette had said about them—which I was pretty certain was mighty little. But once again I had that cold fear that Macartney might have found out something about the seal she had put on all our gold, or her talking to Collins in the dark, for the question Dudley flung at me was just what I had been expecting:

"You didn't see anything of Dunn or Collins between here and Caraquet—or hear from Billy Jones that they'd gone by the Halfway?"

"No," I fenced with a bland, lying truth. "I saw two of our teamsters at the Halfway!"

Dudley shook his head. "Not them—I knew about them! But Dunn and Collins cleared out the day you left, and I thought—" he broke off irrelevantly. "What the dickens possessed you to take Paulette with you that night? She might have been killed—I heard you'd the dog's own trouble on the road!"

That something inside me stiffened up. Whatever he'd heard, I was pretty certain was not all; and I was hanged if I were coming out with the full story of that crazy drive till I knew whether Paulette came into it. I had no desire to talk before Macartney either, in spite of what he might have found out, or guessed; no matter what Paulette might have been mixed up in I was not going to have a stern-faced, set-eyed Macartney put her through a catechism about it. Or Dudley either, for that matter. I had no real voucher for the terms he and Paulette were on, except Marcia's word; and Dudley was no man to trust not to turn on a girl.

"We shot a few wolves, if that's what you mean," I said roughly. "I don't see why that should have worried you about Miss Paulette—or what it has to do with Dunn and Collins!"—which was a plain lie.

"Few wolves! I know all about them!" Dudley retorted viciously. "Billy Jones's wife came out with the plain truth—that you'd been chased by a pack! And as for what Dunn and Collins had to do with my worrying about the gold you carried, it's simple enough. They—" but he stopped, chewing two fingers with a disgusting trick he had. "By gad," he looked up suddenly, "I believe it was them the wolves were after to begin with, Stretton—before they got started on you! And it wasn't what they left La Chance for!"

"What d'ye mean?"

Dudley was chewing his fingers again, but Macartney answered with his usual set-eyed openness. "The gold," he supplied. "I got an idea those two deserters might have laid up beside the Caraquet road somewhere, to wait for you and get it. I had trouble with them over some drilling the morning you left; and when I went back to the stope after seeing you and Miss Paulette off, they'd cleared out. They must have gone a couple of hours before you did. They let out something about hold-ups while I was having the trouble with them, and Wilbraham and I got worried they might have managed to get over the road before you, and be lying up for you somewhere."

"They only left—two hours before I did," said I, with flat irrelevance. I must have stared at Macartney like a fool, but he had knocked the wind clean out of me as to Collins having been the man in the swamp. With only two hours' start neither he nor Dunn, nor any man, for matter of that, could have legged it over my road in time to lie up in the only place I knew someone had laid up—on the corduroy road.

"Well, they didn't get me, and I never saw them," I began—and suddenly remembered that ghastly noise, like the last flurry of a dog fight, that had halted the wolves on my track. My first thought of it, and of Dunn and Collins, had been right. "By gad, I believe I heard them though," I exclaimed, "and if they were on that road they're killed and eaten! But I didn't have any trouble about the gold."

It was true to the letter, for my side had attended to all the trouble, if my side was only a girl who would not have shot without need. But when I explained the noise that might have accounted for Dunn and Collins, Dudley shook his head.

"They didn't get eaten; not they! And your having no trouble with the gold isn't saying you won't have any. If no one saw Dunn and Collins going out to Caraquet I bet they're laid up somewhere on your road yet, waiting for your next trip! And as if that wasn't worry enough, poor old Thompson has to go out of his mind and come back here to be found dead—and I mean to find out how!" He was working himself up into one of his senseless rages, and he turned on Macartney furiously. "You knew him before I did! Write to his people and find out how he got here, anyhow. I'm not going to have any man come back, and just be found dead like a dog, if it is only old Thompson! I'm going to have him traced from the time he left Montreal."

"He had no people," said Macartney blankly. "As far as I know, he was just a bit of driftwood. And as for finding out anything about his journey here, I don't suppose we ever can! All we'll get at was that he came back—and was found dead." And something made me look past him and Dudley, sitting with their backs to the living-room door, and the blood jumped into my face.

Paulette Brown stood in the doorway, motionless, as if she had been there some time. I didn't know if she were merely knocked flat about the wolves and Collins, or scared Macartney might have found out something about her. But she was staring at Macartney's unconscious back as you look at a chair or anything, without seeing it, and if he were pale she was dead white—except her mouth that was arched to a piteous crimson bow, and her eyes that looked dark as pools of blue ink. But she did not speak of Dunn or Collins.

"Do you mean Thompson's been found dead?—the quiet man who was here when I came?" she stammered, as if it choked her. And I had an ungodly fright she was going to say she must have shot him on the corduroy road!

"Billy Jones found him drowned in Lac Tremblant; it was an accident," I exclaimed sharply, before she could come out with more about shooting and wolf bait, and perhaps herself, than I chose anyone to know—till I knew it first. And I saw the blood flash into her face as it had flashed into mine at the sight of her.

"Oh, I thought Mr. Macartney meant he'd been—murdered," she returned faintly. "I'm glad—he wasn't. But if he had been, I suppose it would be sure to come out!"

"Crime doesn't always come out, Miss Paulette," said Macartney.

But Paulette only answered listlessly that she was not sure, one never could tell; and moved to her usual seat by the fire.

I was knocked endways about Collins; for who could have been on the corduroy road if he had not. I would have given most of the world for ten minutes alone with my dream girl and explanations. But Dudley began the whole story of Thompson over again, and Macartney stood there, and Marcia—whom I had not seen since she went to bed with a swollen face—came in, dressed in her hideous green tweed, and stood on tiptoe to chuck me under the chin, with a "Hullo, Nicky, you're back again!"

There was no earthly hope of speaking to my dream girl alone. I shoved the mystery of Collins into the back of my head and went off to my room before I remembered I was still unconsciously holding that torn-off flap of poor old Thompson's envelope in my shut fist. I dropped it on my floor—and grabbed it up again, to stare at it for a full minute. Because there was writing on *it*, too.

"For God's sake, search my cards—my cards—my cards," Thompson had scrawled across the three-cornered envelope flap Macartney's grab had left in my hand: and, knowing Thompson, it was pitiful. He was the sort who must have been crazy indeed before he spoke of the Almighty and cards in the same breath.

I remembered taking his measly solitaire pack out of his pocket at the Halfway, and wished I had brought them along with me. But it was simple enough to go and get them from Billy Jones. Meantime I had no desire to speak to Macartney of them or the scrawled, torn-off flap from Thompson's envelope: he was sick enough already about old Thompson's aberration, without any more proofs of it. It hurt even me to remember I had always laughed at the poor devil and his forlorn cards. I had no heart to burn the scrap of his envelope either, while old Thompson lay unburied. I put it away in my letter case, and locked it up.

Which seemed a tame ending; I had not sense enough to know it was not tame at all!

# CHAPTER 9

## TATIANA PAULINA VALENKA!

Poor old Thompson seemed a closed incident. There was nothing to be found out about him, even regarding his departure from La Chance. Nobody remembered his going through Caraquet, or even the last time he had been there. He was not a man anyone would remember, anyhow, or one who had made friends. We put a notice of his death and the circumstances in a Montreal paper, and I thought that was the end of it all, till Dudley, to my surprise, stuck obstinately to his idea of tracing Thompson from Montreal. He told Macartney and me that he had written to a detective about it, and I think we both thought it was silly. I know I did; and I saw Macartney close his lips as though he kept back the same thought. But we gave old Thompson the best funeral we could, over at the Halfway, with a good grave and a wooden cross. All of us went except Marcia. She said she had never cared about the poor old thing, and she wasn't going to pretend it.

It was a bitter day, with no snow come yet. Macartney looked sick and drawn about the mouth as he stood by the grave, while Dudley read the prayers out of Paulette's prayer book. I saw her notice Macartney when I did, and I think neither of us had guessed he had so much feeling. I stayed a minute or two behind the others, because I'd ridden over, instead of driving with them; and just before I started for La Chance I remembered that torn scrap of paper in my room there. I turned hastily to Billy Jones.

"Those solitaire cards of Thompson's," said I, from no reason on earth but that to find them had been the last request of the dead man, even if it did sound crazy. "I'd like them!"

Billy nodded and went into his shack. Presently he came out and said the cards were gone. He thought he'd put them away somewhere, but they weren't to be found. It was strange, too, because he remembered replacing them in their prayer-book sort of case after he'd spread them by the stove to dry with Thompson's clothes. But his wife said she would find them and send them over. Which she never did, and I forgot them. Goodness knows I had reason to.

I did an errand instead of going straight home from Thompson's funeral that took me into the bush not far from where the boulder had been placed on my road. It was there or near by I had heard wolves pull down a man or men; and after I'd tied my horse and done a little looking around, I found the spot. It was not the scattered bones of two men that sickened me, or even that the long thighs and shanks of one of them were the measure of Collins. It was the top of a skull, with the hair still on it. I did not need the face that was missing. Dunn, with his eternal chuckle, had had stubbly fair hair without a part in it, clipped close till it stood on end—and the same fair hair was on the top of the skull that lay like a round stone in the frozen bush. Whether the two had set out to rob me I didn't know. I did know they had not done it, and that the man Paulette had shot at in the swamp was more of a mystery than ever.

The ground was too hard to do any burying. I made the bones into a decent heap and piled rocks into a cairn over them. If I said a kind of a prayer, too, it was no one's business but that of the God who heard me; the boys had been young, and they were dead while I lived, which was enough to make a man pray. I felt better when I had done it.

But when I got home to La Chance the bald story I told Dudley was wasted. He swore I was a fool, first, for burying two skulls with no faces and imagining they belonged to Dunn and Collins; and next that they were still alive and meaning to run a hold-up on us. From where, or how, he couldn't say. But he kept on at the thing; and the minute he had half a drink in him— which was usually the first thing in the morning—he began to worry me to go out and find where they were cached and hike them out of it; and he kept at it all day. That would not have worried me much since it was only Dudley, and Macartney and the others believed my story; but everything else at La Chance began to go crooked, and everyone's nerves got edgy. Marcia was unpleasantly silent, except when Macartney was there, when she sat in his pocket and they talked low like lovers—only that I was always idiotically nervous they might be talking about Paulette Brown. That was seldom enough though, for half the time Macartney never showed up, even for meals. He was working like ten men over the mine, and good, solid, capable work at that. Whatever had made poor Thompson send him to us he was worth his weight in the gold he was getting out of La Chance in— Well, in chunks! Which was one of the reasons he had to work so hard, and brings me to the naked trouble at La Chance.

We were deadly short of men. Not only were Dunn and Collins dead, but their grisly end seemed to have scared the others. Not a day went by that three or four of them did not come for their time, chiefly rockmen and teamsters—for we had no ore chute at La Chance. Macartney thought it was Dudley's fault, for nagging around all the time, and was sore over it. Dudley said it was Macartney's, though when I pressed him he said, too, that he did not know why. The men I spoke to before they left just said they'd had enough of La Chance, but I could feel a sulky underhand rebellion in the bunk house.

I ran the ore hauling as best I could, and Macartney doubled up the work in the mill. The ore-feeder acted as crusher-man, too, the engineer was his own fireman, which, with the battery man and the amalgamator, brought the mill staff down to four—but they were the best of our men. The others Macartney turned to with the rockmen, and in the course of a fortnight he got a few more men from somewhere he wrote to outside. They were a rough lot; not troublesome, but the kind of rough that saves itself backache and elbow grease. Personally, I think they would not have worked at all, if Macartney had not put the fear of death in them. I caught him at it, and though I did not hear what he said in that competent low voice of his, there was no more lounging around and grinning from our new men. But the trouble among the old men kept on till we had none of them left except the four in the mill. It did not concern me particularly, except that I had to work on odd jobs that should not have concerned me either, and I did not think much about it. What I really did think about—and it put me out of gear more than anything else at La Chance—was Paulette Brown!

It had been all very well to call her my dream girl and to think I'd got to heaven because she'd taken the trouble to drive to the Halfway with me and fight wolves. But she had hardly spoken to me since. And—well, not only the bones and skull I'd buried had smashed up my theory that it was only Collins who'd meant to hold up my gold, but I'd smashed it up, for myself, for a reason that made me wild: Paulette Brown, whose real name Marcia swore was something else, was still meeting a man in the dark! Where, I couldn't tell, but I knew she did meet him; and naturally I knew the man was not Collins, or ever had been. I did my best to get a talk with her, but she ran from me like a rabbit. I was worried good and hard. For from what I'd picked up, I knew the man she met could be nobody at La Chance—and any outsider who followed a girl there likely had a gang with him and meant business, not child's play like Collins.

The thing was serious, and I had no right to be trusting my dream girl and keeping silence to Dudley, but I went on doing it. There is no sense in keeping things back. I was mad with love for her, and if she had given me a chance I would have brushed Dudley out of my way like a straw. I had to grip all the decency I had not to do it, anyway. But if you think I just made an easy resignation of her and sat back meekly, you're wrong. I sat back because I was helpless and too stupid to formulate any way to deal with the situation. I don't know that I was any more silent than I always am, though Marcia said so. I did get into the way of pretending to write letters in the evenings, while Marcia and Macartney talked low, and Dudley went up and down the room in his eternal trudge of nervousness, throwing a word now and then to Paulette seated sewing by the fire—that I kept my back to so that the others could not see my face.

But one night, nearly a month after Thompson was buried, I came in after supper, and Paulette was in my usual place. She was writing a letter or something, and Dudley was preaching to Macartney about the shortage of men in the bunk house. Marcia, cross as two sticks because she was only there to talk to Macartney herself, had Paulette's seat by the fire. I sat down by the table where Paulette was writing, more sideways than behind her.

If I had chosen to look I could have read every word she was writing. But naturally I was not choosing to, for one thing, and for another my eyes were glued to her face. Something in the look of her gave me a sick shock. She was deadly pale, and under the light of Charliet's half-trimmed lamp I saw the blue marks under her eyes, and the tight look round the nostrils that only come to a woman's face when she is fighting something that is pretty nearly past her, and is next door to despair. She looked hunted; that was the only word there was for it. It struck me that look must stop. If I had to march her out into the bush with me by force next morning, I meant to get a solitary talk with her; find out what her mysterious business was at La Chance with a man who had laid up for our gold; and, with any luck, transfer the hunted look to the face of the man who was hounding her—for I felt certain he was still hanging around La Chance.

After that—but there could be no after that to matter to me, with a dream girl who scooted to Dudley every time I tried to speak to her! I took a half-glance at him, and it was plain enough he would be no good to her in the kind of trouble that was on now. If I couldn't have her—since she didn't want me—I was the only person who could help her. She was angel-sweet to Dudley, heaven knows, and he was charming to her when he was himself. When he was not, he had a patronizing, half-threatening way of speaking to her, as if he knew something ugly about her, as Marcia had insinuated, that made me boil. She never resented it either, and that made me boil too. If I had ever seen her even shrink from him, I don't know that the curb bit I had on myself would have held. I wished to heaven she *would* shrink and give me a chance to step in between her and a man who might love her, as Marcia said, but who loved drink and drugs better, or he would not have been talking between silliness and sobriety, as he was that night. And I was so busy wishing it that Marcia spoke to me three times before I heard her.

"Nicky, do make Dudley shut up," she repeated, "he won't let anyone else speak! He's been preaching the whole evening that Collins and Dunn aren't dead, only laid up somewhere round and making the other men desert, and you ought to go and find them—and now he's worrying us about that old idiot Thompson, who got himself drowned! For heaven's sake tell him no one would have bothered to murder the old wretch!"

"Nobody ever thought he was murdered, and I buried Dunn and Collins right enough," said I absently, with my thoughts still on Paulette. But Dudley whisked around on me.

"Marcia's talking rot," he exclaimed, his little pig's eyes soberer than I expected. "I don't mean about those two boys, for I bet they're no more dead than I am, and it would be just like them to lie low and set up a smothered strike among the men as soon as you were ass enough to be taken in by some stray bones! But I do mean it about Thompson. There's no sense in saying there was nothing odd about the way he came back and was found dead—because there was! It was natural enough that the police couldn't trace him in Montreal, for I hadn't a sign of data to give them: but it's darned unnatural that *I* can't trace him in Caraquet. I've sieved the whole place upside down, and nobody ever saw Thompson after he left Billy Jones's that morning on his way to Caraquet!"

Macartney stared at him for a minute; then he put down the pipe he was smoking. "If I thought that, I'd sieve the whole place upside down, too," he said so quietly that I remembered Thompson had been his best friend, and that he had looked deadly sick beside his grave. "But I don't. What it comes to with me is that no one remembers seeing Thompson in Caraquet that particular time, but no one says he wasn't there!"

"Then where's the—" But Dudley checked himself quick as light. If I had been quite sure he was himself I should have been curious about what he had meant to say. But all he substituted was: "Well, nobody remembers seeing him that day, anyway, except Billy Jones!"

"Seems to me that narrows poor Thompson's potential murderers down to Billy Jones," said Macartney ironically, since Billy Jones would not have murdered the meanest yellow pup that ever walked, and Macartney knew it as well as I did. But Dudley made the two of us sit up.

"Who's to say he didn't?" he demanded. "What darned thing do we know about him to say that he mightn't have waylaid poor old Thompson for what money he had on him, and kept him shut up till he had a chance to say he found him drowned?"

Macartney and I stared at each other. The very thought was so monstrous that it must have struck him, as it did me, that it was born of Dudley's drugs and not his intelligence. But it had to be stopped, or heaven knew whom Dudley would be accusing next.

"For God's sake, Wilbraham, shut up," said Macartney curtly. "You make me sick. Isn't it enough to have the old man dead, without saying innocent people killed him!"

"Yes, if they are innocent," Dudley returned so quietly that it surprised both of us. "But I tell you this, Macartney, and Stretton too—if anyone within a hundred miles of this mine did murder Thompson, Billy Jones or anyone else, it'll come out!" and he jerked his head around. "Don't you think so, Paulette?"

"I? I never thought of poor old Thompson having been murdered!" She answered as if she were startled, but she did not turn. "If he was murdered I pray God it will be found out," she added unexpectedly. She had made two false starts at her letter and torn them up, but she had evidently finished it to her liking now, for she sat with the pen poised over the blank end of the sheet to sign her name. Yet she did not sign it. She only sat there abstractedly, with her hand lifted from the wrist.

"There, you see," Dudley crowed triumphantly. "Paulette's no fool: it's facts she and I are after, Macartney. Why, you take the history of crimes generally—murders—jewel robberies—kidnapping for money—half of them with not nearly so much to them as this thing about Thompson—they're always found out!"

"If you're going to talk this rubbish, I'm going to bed," Marcia burst out wrathfully. I saw her pause to catch Macartney's eye, but for once his set gaze was on the floor. She got up, which I don't think she had meant to do, and flounced out of the room. I had no idea I was going to be deadly thankful.

Macartney answered Dudley as the door shut behind her. "I don't know that crimes are always found out, in spite of your faith—and Miss Paulette's," he argued half crossly. "I could remind you of one or two that weren't. What about the Mappin murder, way back in nineteen-five? And that emerald business at the Houstons' country house this spring, with that dancing and circus-riding girl who used to be at the Hippodrome—the Russian, who did Russian dancing on her horse's back? What was her name? I ought to remember. I knew a poor devil of a cousin of hers out in British Columbia who was engaged to her when it happened, and he talked about her enough. Oh, yes, Valenka! She had a funny Christian name too, sort of half Russian, only I forget it. But when that Valenka girl got away with an emerald necklace from the Houstons' house no one ever found out how it was done! You must have heard about her, Stretton?"

I had. Every one had: Macartney need not have troubled to hunt his memory for her Christian name, though it had only reached me in the wilderness through a stray New York paper. But before I could say so Dudley burst out with the same truculence he had used about Billy Jones:

"What d'ye mean Stretton must have heard?"

"Only that Mrs. Houston took a fancy to Valenka and had her down to ride and dance at a weekend party at her house in Long Island; that on Sunday morning, Jimmy Van Ruyne, one of the guests, was found in Valenka's room, soaked with morphine and robbed—not only of the cash in his pocket in the good old way, but of an emerald necklace he had just bought at Tiffany's; and that, to this day, no one has ever laid eyes on that necklace nor on Valenka. She's free and red-handed somewhere, if no one ever found out who railroaded her and Van Ruyne's emeralds out of the United States!"

What sent Dudley into a blazing rage was beyond me. But he fairly yelled at Macartney.

"Free she may be, but when you say 'red-handed' you say a lie! If Jimmy Van Ruyne was fool enough to think so, it was because no Van Ruyne ever could see a. b. spelled ab. D'ye know him? Well," as Macartney shook his head, "he's a rotter, if ever there was one! Got more money than he knows what to do with and always chasing after women. As for Valenka, if you think she came out of a circus and was fair game, that's a lie, too! She was a lady, born and bred. Her mother was American, a Miss Bocqueraz; and her father was one of the best known men in Petrograd, and *persona grata* with one of the Grand Dukes till he got into some sort of political disgrace and died of it. His daughter came to America and danced and rode for her living. First because she was beggared; and second because she'd been taught dancing in the Imperial School at Petrograd and riding in the Grand Duchess Tatiana's private ring for *haute manége*; and was a corker at both. She called herself plain Valenka, and Jimmy Van Ruyne went crazy about her—though Mrs. Houston didn't know it, or she never would have asked the nasty little cad to a spring weekend party."

"To lose an emerald necklace and be stabbed and drugged," commented Macartney drily. "Oh, I'm not saying the Valenka girl wasn't a marvellous sight on a horse! But what Van Ruyne told the police was that he gave his string of emeralds to her on the Saturday afternoon, and got a note from her just after dinner saying that she returned them; only the case—in the time-honored method this time—was empty when he opened it! He was blazing. He went straight up to Valenka's room when he found it out, which was at two in the morning, and said he wanted his emeralds; and she flew at him with a dagger. After which he knew nothing at all till a servant came in at eight and found him lying unconscious in her empty room that she'd just walked out of with his emeralds in her pocket. And no one's ever laid eyes on her, or on Van Ruyne's emeralds ever since."

"That's what Van Ruyne says," Dudley began hotly—and went on in a different voice. "The Valenka girl never stole his emeralds! She may have cut him across the wrist with one of those knife-things women will use for paper cutters; I don't say she didn't. Any girl would have been justified when a man forced his way into her bedroom—for I bet Van Ruyne didn't let out the whole story of that, if he did let out that he bullied her when he found her alone! And he didn't lay any stress, either, on the fact that he was found with the cut artery in his wrist—that was all the stabbing that ailed him—bound up as a surgeon would have done it; or that he'd been given just enough morphine to keep him from wriggling off his bandage and bleeding to death before anybody came: not Van Ruyne!"

"All that doesn't explain how Valenka got away—or what became of her," said Macartney obstinately. "That's the mystery I began on."

I was bored stiff with the whole thing. And whether she had Van Ruyne's emeralds or not I saw no particular mystery in the Valenka girl's disappearance: she had probably had someone outside who had taken her clear away in a motor car. I said so, more because Dudley was glaring at Macartney like a maniac than anything else. And Dudley caught me up short. "I won't have either of you say one more word about Valenka in my house. She was as good as she was pretty; and if someone helped her away she—deserved it!"

There was something so like honest passion in the break in his voice that involuntarily I glanced at Paulette, to see if by any chance she was startled at Dudley's evidently intimate knowledge of a girl none of us had even heard him speak of—and it took every bit of Indian quiet I owned not to stare at her so hard that Dudley and Macartney must have noticed. She was listening, as motionless as if she were a statue. Her lifted hand still held her pen poised over her unfinished letter; but it was rigid, as the rest of her was rigid. Whether it was from anger, surprise, or jealousy of Dudley, I had no idea, but she sat as if she had been struck dumb. And suddenly I was not sure if she were perfectly collected—or absolutely abstracted. For—without even a glance to show she felt my eyes on her—the carved lines of her poised hand fell to the level of her wrist that lay flat on the table, and she began to write the signature to her unfinished letter. I could see every separate character as she shaped it; and with the blazing enlightenment of what she set down on paper only a merciful heaven kept my wits in my skull and my tongue quiet in my head.

For the signature she wrote as plainly as I write it now was not Paulette Brown. It was Tatiana Paulina—that "odd Christian name, half Russian too," of the dancing circus-rider, that no one had ever mentioned—*Tatiana Paulina Valenka*!

# CHAPTER 10

## I INTERFERE FOR THE LAST TIME

*"Must I go now—in the moonlight clear?*
*Would God that it were dark,*
*That I might pass like a homeless hound*
*Men neither miss nor mark."*
—The Ransom.

Tatiana Paulina Valenka!

I sat as still as if I had been stabbed. It was no wonder she had laughed when I asked her if she could ride, no wonder I had thought she moved like Pavlova. Paulette Brown, whom Dudley had brought to La Chance, was Tatiana Paulina Valenka, who had or had not stolen Van Ruyne's emeralds! But the blood sprang into my face at the knowledge, for—by all the holy souls and my dead mother's name—she was my dream girl too! And I believed in her.

All the same, I was thankful Marcia had flounced out of the room before Dudley let loose. It was no wonder she had thought she had seen Paulette Brown before. The wonder was that she had ever forgotten how she had seen her—dancing at the Hippodrome on her four horses as no girl ever had danced—or forgotten the story about her that she had said was "peculiar"! If Marcia's eyes had fallen on the signature mine were on now, I knew her first act would have been to write to Jimmy Van Ruyne; that even if she had only heard Dudley defending an ostensibly absent Valenka she would have written—for Marcia was no fool. Then and there I made up my mind that Marcia should never guess the whole of what she already half-guessed about Paulette Brown; there were ways I could stop *that*.

As for Dudley— But a sudden tide of respect for Dudley, in spite of his drink and all his strangeness, rose flood-high in me. It had been Dudley, of course, who had got Paulette away—for I could not think of her as Tatiana Paulina. How, I did not know; I knew he had not been one of the Houstons' weekend party; but he had done it somehow, and spirited Paulette out to La Chance. As for the rest, a fool could have told that he respected and believed in her. If it had been risky bringing Marcia out into the wilderness with her, it had been clever too, because it was so bold that Marcia had never suspected it. Even I never would have, if Macartney had not brought up Miss Valenka's name. I knew he had done it merely to get Dudley off his cracked idea that Billy Jones might have murdered Thompson, but I was suddenly nervous that Dudley's fool vehemence over a missing girl might have set Macartney on the track of things—and heaven knows that, except he was a competent mine superintendent, I knew little enough how far it would be safe to trust Macartney. But suddenly one thing I did know flashed over me. Macartney and Marcia were a firm, or going to be; and I was instantly scared blue that he might turn around and see that name Paulette Brown had signed to her letter, lying plain under the living-room lamp! I knew I had to wake Paulette up to what she had done and shut up Dudley before he let out any more intimate details the public had never known, like Van Ruyne's bandaged wrist. I yawned and got up, with one hand on the table, and my forefinger pointing straight to that black signature of Tatiana Paulina Valenka that ought to have been Paulette Brown.

"I'm like Marcia, Miss Paulette; I'm going to bed unless you can turn off Dudley's eloquence. Oh, I'm so sorry—I'm afraid I've blotted your letter," I said. I tapped my finger on it soundlessly—and she looked down—and saw!

I said once before that my dream girl had good nerves; she had iron ones. I need not have been afraid she would exclaim. She said quite naturally: "No, it's all right. And it wasn't a letter, anyhow. It was only something I wanted to make clear." She picked it up, folded it small, gathered up the bits of paper she had written on and torn up, and turned round to Dudley. "What are you talking about all this time?"

But if her glance warned him to hold his tongue, as heaven knows her mere presence would have warned me, Dudley was too roused to care. "I was talking about that liar, Van Ruyne," he said, glaring at Macartney.

"He may be a liar, all right," said Macartney rather unpleasantly. "Only, if that Valenka girl didn't steal his emeralds, Mr. Wilbraham, who did?"

"That cousin of hers you said you knew; Hutton, or whatever you said his name was," Dudley retorted, like a fool, for Macartney had never mentioned the man's name. "How, I don't know, but I'm certain of it. He was more in love with her than Van Ruyne, and more dangerous, for all you say he was a good sort. Why, he was the kind to stick at nothing. Miss Valenka had had the sense to turn him down hard; and I believe he stole that necklace of Van Ruyne's from her during the short time she had it—either just to get her into trouble and be revenged on her, or to get her into his power. Whichever it was—to blackmail her—for he'd cadged on her for money before her father died—or to scare her into going to him for help—I'd like to hunt the worthless hound down for it. And I'd never stop till I got him!"

"Like poor old Thompson's murderer," Macartney commented rather drily, "and with no more foundation." But the thought of Thompson seemed to have brought his self-command back to him; he tried to smooth Dudley down. "I don't honestly believe old Thompson could have been murdered," he said gently, "or that Miss Valenka's cousin could have stolen those jewels, for any reason. He seemed a pretty good sort when I knew him in British Columbia. He was a clever mining engineer, too."

"He might have been the devil for all I care! Only if ever I come across him I'll get those emeralds out of his skin," Dudley exploded. Paulette gave one glance at him. It would have killed me; but even Dudley saw how he was giving himself away to a stranger.

"Why under heaven do you work me up about abstract justice, Macartney?" he growled. "You know how I lose my temper. Talk about something else, for goodness sake!"

"Not I—I'm going to bed," Macartney returned casually. Dudley always did work himself up over things that were none of his business, and the Valenka argument evidently had not struck his superintendent as anything out of the ordinary. He nodded and went out. Paulette strayed to the fireplace, and I saw her handful of papers blaze up before she moved away. I was thankful when that signature of Tatiana Paulina Valenka was off the earth, even if Macartney had gone out of the room. Paulette said good night, and went out on his heels.

I heard Macartney ask her something as she passed him where he stood in the passage, getting on his coat to go over to the assay office, where he slept. I thought it was about Marcia, from the tone of his voice, and from Paulette's answer, cursory and indistinct through the closed door: "I know. I'm going to." She added something I could not hear at all, but I heard Macartney say sharply that tomorrow would be too late.

Paulette said "yes," and then "yes" again, as though he gave her a message. Then she spoke out clearly: "There's nothing else to say. I'll do it now." I heard her move away, I thought to Marcia's door. Macartney went out the front door, banging it.

I had no desire to go to bed. I felt as if I had walked from Dan to Beersheba and been knocked down and robbed on the way. I knew my dream girl was not mine, now or ever, because she was Dudley's, but I had never thought of her being anything like Tatiana Paulina Valenka. It was not the jewel story that hit me: I knew she had not stolen Van Ruyne's old necklace, no matter how things looked. It was that she must care for Dudley, or she would never have let him bring her out here. And another thing hit me harder still, and that was Hutton—the cousin Macartney said was engaged to her, and Dudley said cadged on her, till he ended by branding her as a thief and getting away with the spoils. And the crazy thought that jumped into my head, without any earthly reason, was that it was just Hutton who had been hounding her at La Chance; that, while I had been addling my brains with suspecting Collins, it was Hutton that Paulette Brown—whose real name was Valenka—had stolen out to meet in the dark!

Once I thought of it, I was dead sure Hutton had followed her to La Chance. I knew from my own ears that she hated and distrusted the man for whom she had once mistaken me, that it was he from whom she had tried to protect my gold; and I wondered with a horror that made me too sick to swear, if it were Hutton himself, and not Dunn nor Collins, who had cached that wolf dope in my wagon! If it were, he had not cared about wolves killing the girl who drove with me, so long as he got my gold. But there I saw I was making a fool of myself, for he could not have known she was going. I steadied my mind on the thing, like you steady a machine.

If Hutton had been hanging around La Chance, either from so-called love, or to get Paulette into a mess with our gold, as Dudley swore he had with Van Ruyne's emeralds, he could not have been seen about the mine—for Macartney would have recognized him and given him away. He must be cached in the bush somewhere, waiting his chance to grab our gold and incriminate Paulette, as common sense told me she expected. I was sure as death he had a gang somewhere, for no outsider would try to run that business alone; Collins and Dunn might have been on their way to join it the night they got scuppered, very likely: they were just devils enough. But if they had started out to meet Hutton at my corduroy road they had never got there, and I was pretty sure the rest of the gang hadn't either, and Hutton—alone—had been scared to shoot at us and give himself away.

That thought assured me of two things. It was Dunn and Collins who had hidden the wolf bait in my wagon, for Hutton could never have done it and reached the corduroy road before us; and Paulette must really hate Hutton savagely, for she must have known whom she was shooting at on my swamp road! That made me feel better—a little—but there was something I wanted to know. I turned on Dudley for it.

"Look here, I never heard anything about Valenka but newspapers' stories, till tonight. But, if you know the inside of the business, how did that cousin Macartney was talking of ever get hold of that emerald necklace? Didn't Macartney imply he was in British Columbia?"

"He was more likely anywhere than where he'd have to work—if he could get money out of a girl," Dudley snapped. "What I think is that he was masquerading as a servant in the Houstons' house—a chauffeur, perhaps—anything, that would let him hang round and drive a girl half wild. He was a plain skunk. I don't know how he managed the thing, but I know he was there in the Houstons' house, somehow, if Paulette doesn't think so"—he forgot all about the Valenka—"and that he took those emeralds; left the girl powerless even to think so; and disappeared. I never saw him; don't even know what he looks like. But if ever I get a chance I'll hand him over to the law as I'd hand a man I caught throwing a bomb at a child!"

I said involuntarily: "Shut up!" I knew it was silly, but I felt as if walls might have ears in a house that sheltered Paulette Brown—though I knew Marcia was in bed and asleep, and there was no one else who could hear. "You're never likely to see him here, anyhow," I added, since I meant to see him myself first, somehow; after which I trusted he was not likely to matter. And I thought of something to change the subject. "What were you going to say tonight about no one having seen poor old Thompson—when you cut yourself off?"

"Oh, that," Dudley replied almost carelessly. "It mayn't amount to anything, and I only shut up because I didn't want Macartney to take the wind out of my sails by saying so. It was just that if Thompson ever went to Caraquet it ought to be simple enough to find the boy who took his horse back to Billy Jones, and—there's apparently no such boy in Caraquet! What set me on Billy Jones first was that he stammered and stuttered about not knowing him, till I don't believe there ever was any such boy. He's never been heard of since, any more than if he'd gone into the ground. And what I want to know is *why*?—if it's all straight about Thompson and Billy Jones!"

I was silent, remembering—I don't know why—the half-dead boy I had carried home to Skunk's Misery. There was no cause to connect him with the return of Thompson's horse to the Halfway, yet somehow my mind did connect him with it, obstinately. I had never really discovered how he had been hurt by a falling tree, and without reason some animal instinct told me the two things belonged together and that they were somehow wrong. But before I could say so, Dudley burst into unexpected speech, his little pig's eyes as fierce as a tiger's: "Look here, Stretton! I'm going to find out who drowned Thompson, and who took Van Ruyne's emeralds—and hand them both over to the law, if I die for it. And when I say that you know I mean it!"

I did. But once more I made no answer, for I thought I heard Marcia in the passage. I am quick on my feet, and I was outside the door before I finished thinking it. But it was not Marcia outside; it was only Macartney. Yet I stopped short and stared at him, for it was a Macartney I had never seen. He was close to the living-room door, just as if he had been listening to Dudley, and his face was the face of a devil. I never want to see set eyes like his again. But all the effect they had on me was to make me furiously angry, and I swore at him.

"What the devil's the matter with you, Macartney? What do you want?"

"My keys," roughly. "I left them somewhere around this passage and I had to come back for them; I couldn't get into my office. As for what's the matter"—he lowered his voice and motioned me some feet away, out of the light from the living-room door—"I heard all Wilbraham said just now, and by gad, the man's crazy! We've got to get him off all that rot about Billy Jones, or anyone else, murdering Thompson; it's stark madness. Both of us know Billy wouldn't murder a cat! And there's another thing, too! I heard all Wilbraham said about that Valenka girl's cousin, and I wish you'd tell him to go slow on it. I was in too much of a rage, or I'd have gone in and told him myself. Dick Hutton was a friend of mine; no matter how much he was in love with a girl who'd got sick of him for Van Ruyne, he wasn't the kind to sneak round the Houstons' house as a servant. I won't let anyone say that with impunity. It's no use my telling Wilbraham so in the state he's in tonight, but you might gently hint it when you've a chance. I wish to heaven he'd give up drink and drugs and being an amateur detective!" He shrugged his shoulders with a complete return to his ordinary manner. "I'm sorry I startled you just now, but I was too cursed angry to say I was here. Oh, there are my keys!" He stooped, picked them up off the floor, and went out with a careless good night.

"Was that Macartney?" Dudley inquired as I went back to him. "I thought he'd gone!"

"Forgot the office key and came back for it." I felt no call to enter on Macartney's embassy regarding Hutton. "Going to bed?"

Dudley gulped down a horn of whisky that would have settled any two men in the bunk house, nodded, and shut the door behind him. I put out the light and sat on in the living room alone, how long I don't know. I had nothing pleasant to think of, either. It was no use my trying to imagine that Tatiana Paulina Valenka was not going to marry Dudley, whatever I had hoped about Paulette Brown. As far as any chance of her loving me was concerned, I had lost my dream girl forever. She was none of my business any more, except that—"By gad, she *is* my business," I thought in a sudden bitter fury, "as far as Hutton and our gold! If I'm right, and he's hiding round here, I'll put a stopper on any more hold-ups. And I'll make good and sure she never goes out to meet him again, too!"

As I swore it I turned away from the dead fire and the dark room, that looked as if we'd all deserted it hours ago, and went Indian-silent into the hallway. And my heart contracted in a hard, tight lump.

The passage was light as day, with the moon full on the window at the end of it. And wrapped in a shawl, with her back to me, stood my dream girl, undoing the front door as noiselessly as I had come into the passage.

I let her do it. The hallway on which Marcia's bedroom door opened, let alone Dudley's, was no place for Paulette Brown and myself to talk. But I was just three feet behind her as she slid around the corner of the shack, toward the bush that lay dark against the cold winter moon. And I rustled with my feet on purpose, so that she turned and saw me, with the moon full on my face.

"You sha'n't do it," I said. I did not know I had made a stride to her till I felt her arm under my hand. "You sha'n't go!"

My dream girl, who had two names and belonged to Dudley anyhow, said nothing at all. She and I, who had really nothing to do with one another, if I would have laid my soul under her little feet, stood still in the cold moonlight, looking inimically into one another's eyes.

# CHAPTER 11

## MACARTNEY HEARS A NOISE: AND I FIND FOUR DEAD MEN

We must have stood silent for a good three minutes. I think I was furious because Paulette did not speak to me. I said, "You're not to go—you're *never* to go and meet Hutton again, as long as you live!" And for the first time I saw my dream girl flinch from me.

"What?" she gasped so low I could hardly hear. "You know that? What am I going to do? My God, what am I going to do?"

"You're coming back into the shack with me!" We were on the blind side of the house for Marcia and Dudley, but we were in plain view from Charliet's window, and I was not going to have even a cook look out and see Paulette talking to a man in the middle of the night. Her despair cut me; I had never seen her anything but valiant before, and I had a lump in my throat. But I spoke roughly enough. "I didn't know the whole of things till tonight, but now I do, you'll have to trust me. Can't you see I mean to do all I can to help you—and Dudley?" If it were tough to have to add Dudley I did it. But I felt her start furiously.

"Dudley?" she repeated almost scornfully. "Nobody can help Dudley but me—and there's only one way! Mr. Stretton, I promise you I'll never ask again, but—for God's sake let me go to meet Dick Hutton tonight!"

"Not blindly," said I brutally. "If you tell me why, perhaps—but we can't talk here. If you'll come into the house and trust me about what you want to do, I may let you go—just this once—if I think it's the right way!"

"I've only half an hour before it's too late—for any way!" But she turned under the hand I had never lifted from her arm.

I led her noiselessly into the office. I was afraid of the living room. Marcia might come back to it for a book or something. No one but Dudley ever went near the office, and he was safely dead to the world, judging from the horn of whisky he had gone to bed on. The place was freezing, for the inside sash was up, leaving only the double window between us and the night; and it was black-dark too, with the moon on the other side of the house. But there were more things than love to talk about in the dark—to a dream girl you would give your soul to call your own, and know you never will. And I began bluntly, "You've never had any reason to distrust me. I've helped you—"

"Three times," sharply. "I know. I've been—grateful."

It was four, counting tonight when I had warned her to hide her signature from Macartney; but I was not picking at trifles. I said: "Well, I've trusted you, too! I knew the first night I came back here that you were meeting some man secretly, in the dark. But it was none of my business and I held my tongue about it; then, and when you met him again—when it was my business."

"Again?" I heard the little start she gave, if I could not see it.

"The night before you and I took the gold out," I answered practically, "when I told you your hair was untidy. I suppose you only thought I knew you had been out of doors, but I heard the man you met leave you and heard you say to yourself that you'd have to get hold of the gold. I didn't know whether you were honest or not then, or when I gave you back your little seal; and not even when you started for Billy Jones's with me. I knew by the time I got there, if I was fool enough to believe it was Collins you were fighting instead of helping. But any fool must see now that Hutton was the only man likely to have followed you out here! I suppose he told you some lie about giving you up for Van Ruyne's necklace, unless you made silence worth while with Dudley's gold?" and her assent made me angry clear through.

"My soul, girl," I burst out, "you balked him about that, even when you knew he'd put that wolf dope in my wagon, and you were risking your life— you put a bullet in him in the swamp—I can't see why you should be worrying to conciliate him by meeting him tonight!"

But she caught me up almost stupidly. "Put a bullet in him? I didn't— you must know I didn't!"

"There was blood in the swamp and on the road!"

I felt her staring at me in the dark. "It wasn't Dick's," she said almost inaudibly. "It must have been someone else's. And—he doesn't know it was he I shot at that night!"

"It might do him good if he did!" I felt like shaking her, if I had not wanted to take her in my arms more. "Can't you see you've no reason to worry about Hutton? If Dudley told the truth tonight, and he stole those emeralds and shifted the crime on to you, it's you who have the whip hand of him!"

"But he didn't," Paulette exclaimed wildly. "He wasn't near the Houstons' house! It's mad of Dudley to think so. I know he believes it, but—oh, it's mad all the same! And even if Dick did take those emeralds—though I can't see how it was possible—it wouldn't clear me! It would only mean he was able to drag me into it, somehow."

"But you never touched the necklace!" For I knew that.

"No," simply, "but I'm afraid of Dick all the more. If he did take it, to get me into his power"—she caught my arm in her slim hands I had always known were so strong—"can't you see he's *got* me?" she said between her teeth, "and that, next thing, he'll get the La Chance gold? If you don't let me meet him tonight I'll be helpless. I— Oh, can't you see I'll be like a rat in a trap?—not able to do anything? I can make him go away, if I meet him! Otherwise"—the passion in her voice kept it down to a whisper—"it's not only that I'm afraid he can make things look as if I stole from Dudley as well as from Van Ruyne: I'm afraid—*for Dudley*!"

The two last words gave me a jar. I would have given most of the world to ask if she loved Dudley, but I didn't dare: I suppose a girl could love a man with a face like an egg, if she owed him enough. But whether she cared for him or not, "By gad, you've got to tell Dudley that Hutton's here," I said roughly, because I was sick with the knowledge that anyhow she did not love me.

"Tell him?" Paulette gasped through the dark that was like a curtain between us. "I've told him twenty times—all I dared. And he wouldn't listen to a word I said. Ask him: he'll tell you that's true!"

I had no doubt it was. Even on business Dudley's brain ran on lines of its own; you might tell him a thing till you were black in the face, and he would never believe it. Lately, between drugs and drink, he was past assimilating any impersonal ideas at all. Macartney was so worried about him that he'd told off Baker, one of his new men, to go wherever Dudley went. I had no use for the man: he was a black and white looking devil and slim as they make them, in my opinion, though Dudley took to him as though he were a long-lost brother luckily—how luckily I couldn't know. But I wasn't thinking about Baker that night.

"We can't worry over Dudley," I said shortly, "he'll have to take care of himself. But you won't be helpless with Hutton, if I meet him tonight—in your place!"

"You? I couldn't bear you to be in it!" so sharply that I winced.

"It won't hurt you to take that much from me!" It wasn't till long afterwards that I knew I'd been a fool not to have said it with my arms round her, while I told her why—but since I didn't do it there's no sense in talking about it. I went on baldly: "I've got to be in it! I'm not concerned with post-mortems and your past. All I know, personally, is that Hutton's hiding somewhere round this mine to hold up our gold shipments and get even with Dudley; and if you'll tell me where to meet him tonight I can stop both—and be saved the trouble of looking for him from here to Caraquet, let alone getting you some peace of mind instead of the hell you're living in."

"Oh, my God," said Paulette, exactly as if she were in church. "I can't take peace of mind like blood-money—I can't tell you where to find Dick, if you don't know now," and I should have known why if I had had any sense, but I had none. "It's no use, Mr. Stretton, I must go to Dick, alone. I—" But suddenly she blazed out at me: "I won't let you see him! And I'm going to him—now. Take your hand off me!"

I tightened it. "You'll stay here! *Please!* And you can't go on preventing me from meeting Hutton, either. What about the first time I take any gold out over the Caraquet road—and he and his gang try a hold-up on me?"

I said gang without thinking, for I was naturally dead sure he had one. But I was not prepared to have the cork come straight out of the bottle. Paulette clutched me till I bit my lip to keep steady.

"His gang's what I'm afraid of—for Dudley," she gasped, which certainly steadied me—like a bucket of ice. "Look here, when first I met Dick, he told me things, to frighten me—that he'd eighteen or twenty men laid up between here and Caraquet—enough to raid us here, even, if he chose. It was because I knew they were waiting somewhere on the road that night that I drove to Billy Jones's with you. It was one of them I shot when we tore through the swamp. But something went wrong with them; either they'd no guns, or they didn't want to give themselves away by shooting when they saw we were ready—I don't know. But anyhow, something went wrong. And Dick was black angry. He—the last time I spoke to him—he wouldn't even tell me what he'd done with his gang; just said he had them somewhere safe, in the last place you or Dudley would ever look for them. Oh, you needn't hold me any more; I've given in; I'm not going to meet Dick tonight. But I had to tell you about his gang, if I can't about him. And listen, Mr. Stretton. I've tried every possible way to get it out of him, but Dick won't even answer when I taunt him for a coward who has to be backed up. I know he has men somewhere, but he won't tell me where they are, or who they are—now. I believe—" but her voice changed sharply. "Those two boys, Dunn and Collins! You don't think Dudley can be right and they *are* still alive—and have joined Dick's gang?"

"They're dead!" I was about sick of Dunn and Collins, and anyhow I was wondering where the devil Hutton's gang could have gone after their fiasco in the swamp. "They may have meant to join Hutton. But I found what the wolves left—and that was dead, right enough!"

"I don't believe they're dead," said Paulette quietly.

I shrugged my shoulders. But I never even asked her why. For suddenly—with that flat knowledge you get when you realize you should have put two and two together long ago—I knew where Hutton's gang was now and always had been. "Skunk's Misery," I thought dumbfounded. "By gad, Skunk's Misery!" For the thing I should have added to the Skunk's Misery wolf dope was my dream of men talking and playing cards under the very floor where I slept in the new hut the Frenchwoman's son had built and gone away from—because it had been no dream at all. I had actually heard real men under the bare lean-to where I lay; and knowing the burrows and runways under the Skunk's Misery houses, I knew where—and that was just in some hidden den under the rocks the new house had been built on—that house left with the door open, ostentatiously, for all the world to see!

I was blazing, as you always are blazing when you have been a fool. But I could start for Skunk's Misery the first thing in the morning and start alone, with my mouth shut. None of our four old men could be spared from the mill, and I had no use for any of Macartney's new ones; or for Macartney either, for he was no good in the bush. As for Dudley, nerves and a loose tongue would do him less harm at home. Besides, any ticklish job is a one-man job and I was best alone: once I got hold of Hutton there would be no trouble with his followers. But I had no intention of mentioning Skunk's Misery to the girl beside me; she was as capable of following me there as of fighting wolves for me, and with no more reason.

"It's late, and neither you nor I are going to meet Hutton tonight," I said rather cheerlessly. "You'd better go to bed."

"I want to say something first," slowly, as if she had been thinking. "What Macartney said tonight—that I was engaged to Dick Hutton when Mr. Van Ruyne said I took those emeralds—wasn't true! I never was engaged to Dick. I was sorry for him once, because I knew he did—care for me. But I always hated him—I can't tell you how I hated him! I didn't think I could ever love any man till—just lately."

It made me sick to know she meant Dudley. I would have blurted out that shrinking from the mere touch of his hand was a strange way to show it; only I was afraid to speak at all, for fear I begged her for God's sake not to speak of love and Dudley to me! And suddenly something banged even that out of my head. "Listen," I heard my own whisper. "Somebody's awake—walking round!"

It was only the faintest noise, more like a rustle than a footstep, but it sounded like Gabriel's trumpet to a man alone in the middle of the night with a girl he had no shadow of right to. If it were Marcia—but I knew that second it was not Marcia, or even Dudley; though I would rather have had his just fury than Marcia's evil thoughts and tongue.

"By gad, it's outside," I breathed. "Look out!" But suddenly I changed my mind on it. There was only one person who could be outside, and that was Hutton, sick of waiting for Paulette and come to look for her. I had no desire for her to see how I met him instead, and my hands found her shoulders in the dark. "Get back, in the corner—and don't stir!" As she moved under my hands the faint sweet scent of her hair made me catch my breath with a sort of fierce elation. The gold and silk of it were not for me, I knew well enough, but at least I could keep Hutton's hands off it. I slipped to the side of the window and stared out into the dark shadow of the house, that lay black and square in the white moonlight. On the edge of it was a man—and the silly elation left my heart as the gas leaves a toy balloon when you stick a pin in it. It was not Hutton outside. It was—for the second time that night—only Macartney!

I stood and stared at him like a fool. It was a good half minute before I even wondered what had brought Macartney out of his bed in the assay office. I watched him stupidly, and he moved; hesitated; and then turned to the house door. My heart gave a jump Hutton never could have brought there. Macartney in the house with a light, coming into the office for something, for all I knew, and finding Paulette and me, would be merely a living telephone to Marcia! I tapped at the office window.

Macartney had good ears, I praised the Lord. He turned, not startled, but looking round him searchingly, and I stuck my head out of the hinged pane of the double window, thanking the Lord again that I had not to shove up a squeaking inside sash. "What's brought you back again?" I kept my voice down, remembering Marcia. "Anything gone wrong?"

"What?" said Macartney rather sharply. He came close and stared at me. "Oh, it's you, Stretton? I thought it was Wilbraham, and he wouldn't be any good. It was you I wanted. I've got a feeling there's someone hanging round outside here."

I hoped to heaven he had not seen Hutton, waiting for an appointment a girl was not going to keep, and I half lied: "I haven't seen anyone. D'ye mean you thought you did?"

Macartney nodded. "Couldn't swear to it, but I thought so. And I'd too much gold in my safe to go to bed; I cleaned up this afternoon. I was certain I glimpsed a strange man slipping behind the bunk house when I went down an hour ago, and I've been hunting him ever since. I half thought I saw him again just now. But, if I did, he's gone!"

"I'll come out!"

But Macartney shook his head sententiously. "I'm enough. I've guns for the four mill men who sleep in the shack off the assay office, and you've a whack of gold in that room you're standing in; you'd better not leave it. Though I don't believe there's any real need for either of us to worry: if there was anyone around I've scared him. I only thought I'd better come up and warn you I'd seen someone. 'Night," and he was gone.

I had a sudden idea that he might be a better man in the woods than I had thought he was, for he slid out of the house shadow into the bush without ever showing up in the moonlight. And as I thought it I felt Paulette clutch me, shivering from head to foot. It shocked me, somehow. I put my arm straight around her, like you do around a child, and spoke deliberately,

"Steady, sweet, steady! It's all right. Hutton's gone by now. Anyhow, Macartney and I'll take care of you!"

"Oh, my heavens," said Paulette: it sounded half as if she were sick with despair, and half as if I were hopelessly stupid. "Take care of me—you can't take care of me! You should have let me go. It's too late now." She pushed my arm from her as if she hated me and was gone down the passage to her room before I could speak.

I shut the office window, with the inside sash down this time, and took a scout around outside. But Macartney was right; if anyone had been waiting about he was gone. I could not find hide or hoof of him anywhere, and the moon went down, and I went in and went to bed. In two minutes I must have been asleep like a log—and the first way I knew it was that I found myself out of bed, dragging on my clothes and grabbing up my gun.

Whatever the row was about it was in the assay office. I heard Macartney yell my name through a volley of shots and knew we had both been made fools of. I had stopped Paulette meeting Hutton, and Hutton had dropped on Macartney and the assay office gold! I shook Dudley till he sat up, sober as I never could have been in his shoes, saw him light out in his pyjamas to keep guard in his own office that Paulette and I had only just left, and legged it for the assay office and Macartney.

I didn't see a soul on the way, except the men who were piling out of the bunk house at the sound of a row, as I had piled out of bed; and I thought Macartney had raised a false alarm. But inside his office door I knew better. The four mill men who slept in the shack just off it were all on the office floor, dead, or next door to it. Their guns were on the floor too, and Macartney stood towering over the mess.

"Get those staring bunk-house fools out of here," he howled, as the men crowded in after me. "I haven't lost any gold, only somebody tried to raid me. Why didn't you come and cut them off when I yelled for you? They—they got away!"

And suddenly, before I even saw he was swaying, he keeled over on the floor.

# CHAPTER 12

## THOMPSON'S CARDS: AND SKUNK'S MISERY

For that second I thought Macartney was dead. But as I jumped to him I saw he had only fainted, and that nothing ailed him but a bullet that had glanced off his upper arm and left more of a gouge than a wound. Why it made him faint I couldn't see, but it had. I left him where he had dropped and turned to the four men he had been standing over. But they were past helping. They were decent men too, for they were the last of our own lot—and it smote me like a hammer that they might have been alive still if I had not interfered with Paulette that night and kept her from meeting Hutton.

I knew as I knew there was a roof over my head that it was he who had fallen on Macartney, and I would have chased straight after him if common sense had not told me he would be lying up in the bush for just that, and all I should get for my pains would be a bullet out of the dark that would end all chance of me personally ever catching Hutton. I took stock of things where I stood, instead. Whether he had a gang or not, I knew he had been alone in the thing tonight, and he had done a capable job. Our four men had been surprised, for they were all shot in the back, as if they had been caught coming in the office door.

Whether Macartney had been surprised or not I could not tell. The revolver he had dropped as he fainted lay beside him empty, and there were slivers out of the doorpost behind the dead men. None of them seemed to have been much help to him. Three had not fired a shot; the fourth had just one cartridge missing from his revolver, where he lay with his face to the door—and I saw it accounted for by a tearing slash in a blue print stuck on the wall to the left of the doorway. I turned to the inside wall to see where the bullet that had glanced off Macartney had landed, and as I swung round he sat up.

"You may well look—it was one of our own men got me," he said thickly, and his curse turned my stomach; I never knew any good come of cursing the dead. I told him to shut up and tell how the thing had happened. And he grinned with sheer rage.

"It was plain damn foolery! I told you I believed I'd seen someone spying around the mine, and after I'd left you I didn't feel so sure that I'd cleared him out. I woke those fools up," his glance at the dead matched his curse at them, "and said if they heard anyone prowling round my door they were to lie low in their own shack, let him get in at me here, and then bundle out and cut him off from behind. And what they did was to lose their heads. They heard someone or they didn't—I don't know. But the crazy fools piled out of their shack and ran in to me; and a man behind them—*behind* them, mind you—came on their heels and plugged every son of them before they were more than inside my door! It was then I yelled for you."

"D'ye mean you saw him—when he shot them?"

"I didn't see what he *looked* like," scornfully, "with four yelling, tumbling men between him and me. But I guess he was the man I'd been looking for. I fired and missed him, and when I lit for him over the men he'd killed he was gone. I emptied my gun into the dark on chance and yelled some more for you, and it was then I got it myself. As I turned around in the doorway, Sullivan," he pointed to the only man whose gun had been fired, "that I thought was *dead*, sat up and let me have it in the arm." He pointed to the ripped blue print. "You see what I'd have got if it had caught me straight! And that's all there was to it."

"D'ye mean"—I bit back Hutton's name. I had no time to hatch up a lie about him, and I was not going to drag in Paulette—"that—whoever was there, never even fired at you?"

"How do I know who he fired at?—I couldn't see inside of his head! I know he *hit* those chumps who could have got him if they had obeyed orders—let alone that if they'd stayed out I'd have got him clean myself when he came in. As it was, he cleared out before I could do it," said Macartney blackly, but the excitement had gone from his voice. "Call a couple of the bunk-house men to carry these four back to their shack and clean up this mess, will you? And come into my room while I tie up this cut. It's no good going after whoever was here now."

I knew that: also that I could get after him better single-handed at Skunk's Misery, where he would not expect me; or I would have been gone already. But I didn't air that to Macartney as I followed him into the partitioned-off corner he called his room. He had the last two clean-ups in his safe there, and he nodded to it as he hauled off his shirt for me to bind up his arm.

"With what's there, and what you and Wilbraham have in his office, we've too much around to be healthy," he observed succinctly, "and I guess someone's got wind of it. I don't know that it'll be any healthier for you to try running it out to Caraquet and get held up on the road! But I suppose it's got to go."

I nodded. I knew it was hand to mouth with Dudley: he had no cash to call on but the mine output, and immediate payments had to be made on the machinery we were using. But I was not excited about being held up on the Caraquet road—after I'd once been to Skunk's Misery. I was not red-hot about hurrying there, either; I wanted to give Hutton time to get back to his lair and feel easy about pursuit after his abortive raid. "I expect we'll worry along," I said idly. "Gimme that clean rag for your arm!"

But Macartney cast down the handkerchief in his hand. "This fool thing's too short! Open that box, will you? There's a roll of bandage just inside."

There was. But there was something else just inside, too. I stared at a worn leather case, that pretended to be a prayer-book with a brass clasp and tarnished gilt edges, a case I had seen too often to make any mistake about. "By gad," I cried blankly. "Why, you've got old Thompson's cards!"

Macartney was poking at his wounded arm, and he winced. "Hurry up, will you? I can't stop this silly blood. Of course I have Thompson's cards; I can't help it if you think I'm an ass. I liked the old man, and I didn't fancy the Billy Joneses playing cribbage with the only thing in the world he cared for. I took the cards the day we buried him—saw them lying in the kitchen."

"I expect you needn't have worried about Billy," I commented absently. "He was going to give those cards to me, only he and I couldn't find them."

"Do come on," snapped Macartney. He was set-eyed as usual, but I guessed he was ashamed to have had me find him out in a sentimental weakness. "I'd have told you I had them if I'd known you cared. You can take the things now, if you want them."

It was not till that minute that I remembered Macartney could not know why I wanted them, nor anything about the sort of codicil I'd torn off the envelope of Thompson's letter to Dudley: for there had been nothing about cards in what he'd read in it, or in the letter itself. But as the remembrance of both things shot up in me, I didn't confide them to Macartney, any more than I had to Dudley himself. I had a strange sort of idea that if Thompson's pencilled scrawl had meant anything more than the wanderings of a distressed mind, I'd better get hold of it myself first. I said: "All right," and pocketed Thompson's cards. Then I did up Macartney's arm, and the two of us went up the road to Dudley. He and his dry nurse, Baker, who'd promptly arrived from the bunk house, stumped straight back to the assay office with Macartney to fuss over the men who'd been killed. I was making for my own room, to see if Thompson's resurrected cards would shed any light on his crazy scrawls, when I heard a poker drop in the living room. Somebody was in there, raking up the fire.

Charliet had gone after Macartney, with Dudley and Baker. I guessed Paulette had got up and was trying to start the fire—for she was always working to keep things comfortable—if I haven't mentioned it—even for me. I once caught her darning my rags of socks and crying over them—the Lord knew why! I went in to stop her now—and it was I who stopped dead in the doorway. It was not Paulette inside: it was Marcia! Marcia in a velvet dressing gown, poking the ashes all over the hearth. I could have sworn I had seen Paulette burn the letter she had signed with Tatiana Paulina Valenka's name, but all the same the look of Marcia's back turned me sick. And her face turned me sicker as she flung around on me, with her fingers all ashes—and Paulette's letter in her hand!

I kept back a curse at the raw fool that was me. I might have seen it was not a tightly folded wad of stiff paper I had watched burn up, but just the light torn scraps Paulette had thrown in with it. What was more, I had been alone with the thing under my very nose in the light ashes into which it must have sunk and never had the sense to burrow for it. It was too late even to snatch for it: Marcia had read it! She held it up to me now—and Tatiana Paulina Valenka, black on the yellow of the scorched paper, hit me on the eyes.

"Who was right, Nicky Stretton?" she demanded triumphantly. "I told you I'd seen *Paulette Brown* before! Only I never thought of the Houston business. I could kill Dudley; how dare he bring me out here with a thief! I won't have her here another day."

"What thief?" I snapped. "I don't know what you mean! Why on earth are you poking in the ashes? What are you up for?"

"Only a Paulette Brown could stay asleep, with Dudley yelling at you and Macartney," scornfully. "But if you want to know what I was poking in the ashes for, I had no matches, and my fire was out, so I came in here for a log to light it up. And I found this!"

"Well, burn it," said I furiously. But she had begun to read it out, and I would have been a fool to stop her, for what Marcia knew I had to know. But it knocked me silly. The something Paulette had "wanted to make clear" was just a letter to Hutton! And the Lord knows it made me more set than ever on getting to Skunk's Misery before Hutton could know that Tatiana Paulina Valenka had given in! Because she had. She was not only going to meet him; she was going away with him, Marcia's hard voice read out baldly, if only he would give up the plan in his head. But it was the last sentence that bit into me:

"Oh, Dick, have some mercy! I know you hate me now, but have some mercy; don't do what I'm afraid of. I'll give you all you want—myself—everything—if only you'll let that be. Go away, as I begged you, and I'll leave Dudley for you, and go too." And it was signed, as I knew Paulette Brown had not meant to sign anything, "Tatiana Paulina Valenka."

I never even wondered how she had meant to get it to Hutton, if she had not supposed she burned it. Every drop of my blood boiled in me with the determination that she should never pay Hutton's price with her lips against his that she hated, and his cheek on her soft hair I had never touched; all the gold Dudley Wilbraham could ever mine was not worth that. But I kept a cold eye on Marcia. "A half-burnt letter—that wasn't going to be sent—isn't anything but girl's nonsense," I swore contemptuously.

"Isn't it? We'll see—when Dudley reads it!" Marcia looked like a devil hunched up in her dressing gown, with her gums showing as she grinned. "I told you she never meant to marry him. Now we'll see if he marries her—when she writes letters like this!"

"I won't let you show it to Dudley!"

"You are like—everybody: cracked about a Paulette Brown!" Marcia retorted; and if I had only known what the "everybody" was going to mean I think I could have managed her, even then, by coming out with it. But I didn't know, and I did the best I could.

"Marcia Wilbraham, if you dare to show that thing to Dudley, or so much as speak of it, I'll pay you out—so help me," I said; and if it was in a voice no decent woman knows a man can use, I meant it to be. It scared Marcia, anyhow, though heaven knew I didn't see how I could ever pay her out, no matter what she did. She let go of the letter, which she had to, for I had her by the wrist. I would have burnt it up, only I had no match. Marcia leaned forward suddenly, electrically, and tapped the "Oh, Dick" in the last sentence, that was the only name in the letter.

"Well, I'm damned," said she coolly. "Why, the thing's to you! Do you mean you're going to run away with that—that girl?"

"No," I said furiously and then saw I was an ass, "I mean, not now!"

"Since I know about you," Marcia cut me off sweetly. But she stared at me calculatingly. "H—m," said she, "I beg your pardon for mistaking your N for a big, big D, Nicky darling, but you see I never heard anyone call you plain, short Nick! I don't exactly see why she had to write with you in the house, either, but you needn't be nervous. I'm not going to use my cinch on you—not now, anyway! I've changed my mind about telling Dudley. It won't do me any harm to keep something up my sleeve against you, if ever I want to do anything you don't admire. It wasn't the least bit of use for you to snatch that letter; I learned it off by heart before you came in on me. And I can always threaten Dudley now that I'll tell who Paulette Brown really is, if he tries to bully me about anyone I have a fancy for!"

Of course I knew she was thinking of Macartney. I didn't believe Dudley would have cared if she had married him ten times over. But he might have been making some unreasonable objection to Macartney, at that, for all I knew.

"I don't care one straw about your knowing I was going to take Paulette Brown out of this. But if you don't hold your tongue on it, I'll know it, so you mind that," I observed with some heat. Yet I was easier. She could not talk that night, anyhow, and she was welcome to come out with her crazy lie about Paulette and myself, once Hutton was dead—because he and a snake would be all one to me, once I got my hands on him. After that I had no qualms about being able to make Dudley see the truth concerning that letter, and that it had been written to save his gold—and his life, likely enough! I let Marcia believe the name in the letter was mine, and that Paulette had been going off with me. All I wished was that she had been. I went off to my room and left Marcia sitting over the dead fire—not so triumphant as she'd meant to be, for all the good face she put on it.

Paulette's letter had pretty well knocked out all the interest I had in old Thompson's cards, but I got out the torn scrap of paper I'd put away. There was nothing on it but what I'd read before: "For God's sake search my cards—*my cards!*"—and it looked crazier than ever with the things in my hand. The cards had been water-soaked and were bumpy and blistery where Billy Jones had dried them, even though they were flattened out again by the pressure of their tight case; but there was nothing *to* them, except that they were old Thompson's beyond a doubt. If I had thought there might be writing on them there was not so much as the scratch of a pencil. There seemed to be a card missing. I thought it was the deuce of hearts; but I was too sick over Marcia's discovery about Paulette to really examine the things and make sure. I shoved them into my coat pocket beside what was there already, just as Dudley came into my room.

He had enough to worry him without hearing that Marcia had found out about Paulette. He sat on my bed, biting his nails; and said—what Macartney had said—that we had too much gold at La Chance to run the risk of losing it by a better organized raid on it: and—what I had known for myself—that the mine output represented his only ready money for notes that were past renewing, and that it had to go out to Caraquet. When I said why not, he bit his nails some more, and said he was afraid of a hold-up: what he wanted me to do was to ride over to the Halfway and scout around from there to clear the Caraquet road, before I started out from La Chance with an ounce of gold.

The idea suited me well enough. It would cover my expedition to Skunk's Misery. But I did not mention that, or Hutton, to Dudley; and never guessed I was a criminal fool! I did not mean to waste any time in scouting around the road, either, when I knew just where my man would be sitting, with the half dozen wastrels he had probably scraped up. But first I wanted five minutes, even two minutes, with Paulette, to warn her of what Marcia knew. So I said the afternoon would be time enough to start.

But Dudley would not hear of it and blazed out till I had to give up all idea of warning Paulette, and get out. And as I rode away from La Chance the last person I saw was Macartney, though I might not have remembered it, if I had not turned my head after I passed and caught the same grin on his face he had worn there the night his own man shot him. I rode back and asked him what the mischief he was grinning at.

"Grinning—because I'm angry," Macartney returned with his usual set stare. "I'd sooner go with you than stay here, burying men and talking to Wilbraham. I'm sick of La Chance, if you'd like to know. I came here to mine, not to play in moving pictures. But I guess I've got to stick, unless I can hurry up my job here. So long—but I don't expect you'll see anything of last night's man on the Caraquet road!"

Neither did I, nor of anyone else. But I was not prepared to find the Halfway stable empty, when I rode in there just at dark. The house was as deserted as the stable, though the fire was alive in the stove, and taking both things together, I decided Billy and his wife had taken a four-horse team into Caraquet for a load. I had meant to borrow one of his horses to go on to Skunk's Misery—for this time I intended to ride there. But with no horse to borrow, there was nothing to do but to ride my own, and it was toward ten that night when I left him to wait for me in a spruce thicket, within half a mile of the porcupine burrows that Skunk's Misery called houses.

As I turned away, the cold bit a hundred times worse for the lack of snow in the woods, and the bare ground made the pat of my moccasins sound louder than I liked; but on the other hand I should leave no track back to my waiting horse, if I had to clear out without getting Hutton. The thought made me grin, for I had no fear of it.

Hutton would be asleep, judging from the look of things; for as I got fairly into Skunk's Misery, it lay still as the dead. The winding tracks through it were deserted; silent between and under the great rocks and boulders; slippery in the open with droppings from the pine trees that grew in and on the masses of huddled rocks. The wind rose a little, too, and soughed in the pine branches, to die wailing among the stones. It did not strike me as a cheerful wind for a man in Hutton's shoes, for it covered the light sound of my feet as I went past the hut of the boy I had nursed and through the maze of tracks his mother had shown me, to the new log lean-to the Frenchwoman's son had built and never used. But, as I reached it, I was suddenly not so sure Hutton was there!

The lean-to looked all right. The door was open, just as I had left it. But, as I crossed the threshold, I knew I was too late, and there was nobody inside, or in the cave underneath it where men had been when I slept there. The place had that empty feeling of desertion, or late occupancy and a cold lair, that even a worse fool than I could not mistake now. I shut the door on myself without sound, all the same; snapped my pocket lantern; and stared—at just what I had known I was going to find.

There was nothing in the place now but the bare lean-to walls and the rock they backed on; but twenty men had been living there since I left it. The black mark of their fire was plain against the rock face; the log floor was splintered by heavy boots with nails in them—which did not speak of the moccasined return of the Frenchwoman's son—and in the place where I had once made a bed of pine boughs and carried it away with me there lay a flurry of litter that spoke volumes: for among it was a corned-beef can that was no product of Skunk's Misery, where meat meant squirrels and rabbits, and—a corked bottle of wolf dope! That I laid gingerly aside till I had poked around in the rest of the mess, but there was not much else there besides kindling. I got up to leg it for the underground cave, blazing that I had missed Hutton and half hoping he might be there—but I dropped flump on my knees again, dumbfounded.

Underneath the displaced litter, stuck sideways in a crack of the log floor, was a shiny, dirty white playing card. I pulled it out. And in the narrow white beam of my electric lantern I saw the missing two of hearts out of Thompson's pack!

I saw more, too, before I even wondered how one of Thompson's cards had ever got to Skunk's Misery. The deuce of hearts was written on—closely, finely and legibly—with indelible pencil. And as I read the short sentences, word by word, I knew Thompson had never got to Caraquet, never got anywhere but to the cave under the very lean-to I knelt in—till he had been brought up from it, here—to be taken away and drowned in Lac Tremblant, as a decent man would not drown a dog! And I knew—at last—where Hutton and his gang were, and who Hutton was!

But I made no move to go underground to the cave to look for them. And the only word that came to my tongue was: "*Macartney!*"

# CHAPTER 13

## A DEAD MAN'S MESSENGER

For the written message on Thompson's lost card was plain. Macartney was—Hutton! And Hutton's gang were just the new, rough men Macartney had dribbled in to the La Chance mine!

It was Macartney—our capable, hard-working superintendent—for whom Paulette had mistaken me in the dark, that first night I came home to La Chance and the dream girl, who was no nearer me now than she was then; Macartney from whom she had sealed the boxes of gold, to prevent him substituting others and sending me off to Caraquet with worthless dummies; Macartney I had heard her tell herself she could not trust; Macartney who had put that wolf dope—that there was no longer any doubt he had brought from Skunk's Misery—in my wagon; Macartney who had had that boulder stuck in the road to smash my pole, by the same men who were posted by the corduroy road through the swamp to cut me off there if the wolves and the broken wagon failed; and Macartney who had been balked by a girl I had left at La Chance to fight him alone now!

The thing seemed to jump at me from six places at once, now that I knew enough to see it was there at all. But what sickened me at my own utter blindness was not the nerve of the man, but just the risk he had let Paulette run on the Caraquet road, and—old Thompson! For Thompson had never sent Macartney to La Chance, and Macartney had had him murdered in cold blood!

If my eyes fogged as I stared at the dead man's two of hearts, it was only half with fury. Old Thompson had been decent, harmless, happy with his unintelligent work and his sad solitaire—and he had been through seven hells before he wrote what I read now:

"Wilbraham—Stretton—pray God one of you saw all I could put inside envelope of last letter Macartney forced me to write. I never sent him to La Chance. I never saw the man till he waylaid me between Halfway and Caraquet, and brought me here. Do not know where it is, am prisoner underground. Wrote you two letters to save my miserable life; know now I have not saved it. Your lives—gold—everything—in danger too. For any sake get Macartney before he gets you. No use to look for me. Tried to warn you inside envelope, but suppose was no use. Good-by. *Take care, take care!* There was a boy Macartney sent off with my horse; was kind; said he would come back. When he does, takes this to you— He has not come. Been brought up into lean-to, am gagged, feel death near. Forgive treachery—life was dear—get Macar—"

But the scrawl broke off in a long pencil line, where death had jerked Thompson's elbow, and his card had fallen from his hand.

I sat on the floor and saw the thing. Macartney, hidden in Skunk's Misery, making plans to get openly and with decent excuse to La Chance, had fallen on Thompson and used him. And for Thompson, writing lying letters in Skunk's Misery in fear of the death that had come to him in the end, there had been no rescue. His scribbled envelope, even if Dudley or I had understood it, had come too late. The boy who took his horse to Billy—whoever he was—had never come back. Thompson had not even had time, in the end, to slip his written-over card into the cased pack I had found in his almost empty pockets, before Macartney's men—for of course Macartney himself had never been near the place since he got his wolf dope there and left it for good—had taken him off and made away with him. Once his last letter was written and posted under cover from Caraquet to be reposted to Dudley from Montreal by some unknown hand, Macartney had no more use for Thompson, and a screen against betrayal on two sides: either by his own men, or that chance finding of Thompson's body that had actually happened; for Thompson's own letter would clear his murderer.

As for Thompson's envelope! It's an easy enough thing to do if you just slip your pencil inside an envelope and write blindly, but it made me sick to think of poor old Thompson scrawling in the inside of his envelope, furiously, furtively, while the ink of his neat copperplate dried on the outside, and Macartney likely stood by poring over the actual letter, wondering if there was any flaw in it that could show out and damn him. And the desperate scrawl in the envelope had been *no good*, thanks to the fool brain and tongue of myself, Nicky Stretton! It had done more to warn Macartney than either Dudley or me, since if Thompson had written in the reverse of the envelope he was also likely to have written on anything that would take a pencil.

It was no wonder Macartney had stood stunned over that envelope, till Dudley and I believed him heartsick for his friend, for it must have been then that he remembered Thompson's cards—that I guessed the old man had just sat and played with, day in and day out, while he was a prisoner and about to die. Thompson could have written on them; and Macartney must have feared it, or he never would have stolen them from Billy Jones. I hoped grimly that he had been good and worried before he got his chance to do it and set his mind at ease. And at ease it must have been, for he had actually known nothing about the cards; he could only have taken them on chance, from sheer terror, and found them harmless. He had probably never even noticed one was missing—and whatever Thompson had not been wise about he had been wise when he took out a deuce, and not one of the four aces the most casual eye must miss—or he would never have let me have them, contemptuously, as one lets a child play with a knife without a blade.

Only I was not so sure this particular knife had no blade—for Macartney!

He knew nothing of the desperate scrawl on the bottom flap of that envelope that his own hasty grab had jerked off and left in my fist; nothing of the deuce of hearts that made its crazy inscription pitifully sane to me now; and nothing in particular about me, Nicky Stretton. But when I came to think of all I knew about Macartney, that was no remarkable consolation; for—except his never noticing that the bottom flap of Thompson's envelope was missing, and taking it for granted it had been blank like the top one—he had made a fool of me all along the line!

I had stopped Paulette from going away with him the night before, after she thought she had burned the note she had meant to slip into his hand; but he must have told her, outside in the passage, when I thought he was sending a message to Marcia, that if she did not go with him then—in the next hour— he would begin trouble that very night for Dudley and La Chance.

And he had! It was Paulette he was waiting for, when he lied to me about a strange man. And he had gone straight down to the assay office, done his own alarm of a robber, and killed four men to give it artistic truth. It was no wonder he had said he was sick of playing in moving pictures and grinned at me when I left La Chance to search the Caraquet road for nobody else but himself.

As for his gang, the very bunk-house men he had told me to order out of the assay office, were just Macartney's own gang from Skunk's Misery, come over when they had silenced Thompson forever; at Macartney's elbow whenever he chose to murder the lot of us and commandeer the La Chance mine. I wished, irrelevantly, that Dunn and Collins *had* got to Macartney, instead of being killed on the way; they might have been chancy young devils about stealing gold, but they would never have stood for murdering old Thompson! It was no good thinking of that, though.

I stowed away Thompson's deuce of hearts, that no boy had ever come for, in the case with those other pitiful cards he had told me to search, and got on my feet with only one thought in my head—to get back to La Chance and my dream girl that Macartney was alone with, except for Dudley—Dudley whom he hated, who had threatened him for Paulette Valenka, for Thompson, till it was no wonder I had found him with the face of a devil where he lurked eavesdropping in the shack hall. And there something else hit me whack. Baker, Dudley's jackal, was one of Macartney's gang: told off, for all I knew, to put him out of the way! I wheeled to get out of that damn lean-to quicker than I had got in; and instead I stood rooted to the floor. *Below me, somewhere underground, somebody was moving!*

Naturally, I knew it could not be Macartney, because he could not have got there, even if he had not had other fish to fry at home. But one of his gang might have been left at Skunk's Misery and could have the life choked out of him. There was no way leading underground directly from the lean-to, or I would have been caught the night I slept there and believed real voices were a dream. I slid out of the door, around the boulder that backed the place, and was afraid of my lantern. I went down on my hands and knees to feel for a track and found one, down a gully that ran in under a blind rock. I crawled down it, all but flat, as I burrowed like a rabbit, with my back scraping against the living rock between me and the sky, and my head turned to the place where I knew the lean-to stood. I was under it with no warning whatever; in a natural, man-high cellar I could stand up in, with half a dozen bolt holes running off it: and I had no need to flash up my lantern to see them. There was a light in the place already from a candle-end Macartney's men must have left behind; and beside it, not looking at me, not even hearing my step, because he was sobbing his heart out, lay the boy I had carried home from the Caraquet road!

"Thompson's boy, who took his horse to Billy—who never came back!" I said to myself. God knows I touched him gently, but he screamed like a shot rabbit till he saw my face.

"You?" said I. "What's the matter with you? Brace up; it's only me!"

Brace up was just what he did not do. He sank back with every muscle of him relaxed. "Bon Dieu, I thought you was him come back," he gasped in his bastard French Indian, "that man that half killed me on the Caraquet road! But it wasn't him I was crying about. It was the other man—that promised me two dollars for something."

"To come back and take a letter—where you had taken his horse?"

The boy—I did not even know his name—nodded, with a torrent of sullen patois. He had never come for his two dollars, and now the man was gone and he would never get it. But it was not his fault. The first man—the one who had sent him to the Halfway with the horse—had caught him crawling back for the letter, had told him the man who was going to pay him had gone away long ago, and had taken him out to chop firewood and let a tree fall on him. How the lad had ever crawled out to the Caraquet road I did not ask. I think the thing that stabbed me was that I had been within five hundred yards of Thompson all the time I was nursing this very boy, that the knowledge of it had lain behind unconscious lips within a hand's breadth of me, that I had gone away ignorant, leaving Thompson robbed of the only help he could ever have had.

"Why didn't you tell me all that—the night I came over to your mother's?" I groaned.

The boy said shortly that his mother would have gone straight off and told I'd been there, if he had come out with the truth. It was all lies she had told me about the Frenchwoman's son; he had never been near the place. It was the man who had half killed him who had built the lean-to, and his mother had said she would finish the business if ever he opened his mouth about it, or let out the truth about the same man sending him to the Halfway with a horse, or the smelling stuff she had helped him make.

"You're sure she didn't go and tell that man about me, anyway?" I remembered Macartney's grin.

But the boy shook his head. "She didn't worry; she said you were too big a fool to matter!" After which wholesome truth he announced listlessly that he was done with his mother. She had turned him out of her house now, anyway. She said he was no good to her, now that he could only crawl, and could not even trap enough rabbits to live on, and she had another man living in her house who would do it for her. So he had come here to find the man who had promised him two dollars—that solitary bill that had been all the money in Thompson's pockets—and when he found him gone and the place empty he had stayed there to hide, and because he had nowhere else to go.

I thought of his mother's haggard, handsome face and hard mouth. Macartney had certainly found a good ally while he was laid up in Skunk's Misery waiting for his chance to fall on Paulette. But all that did not matter now. What did matter was that I had found the missing link between Thompson's cards and Macartney in the boy who had taken Thompson's horse back to the Halfway. I had no mind to produce him now though; for there were other things to be looked to than showing up old Thompson's murder. And the boy was safe where he was, for one glance at him had told me he could not walk half a mile.

"Are you safe from your mother here—and can you get food for yourself?" I demanded abruptly, and the boy nodded the head I knew would never be other than a cripple's. "Well, you stay here," I told him, because if ever I needed the poor little devil for a witness against Macartney he would be no good lying dead somewhere in the bush, "and I'll come back and pay you ten times two dollars for just waiting here till I come. But you'll have to hide if that man comes back who sent you out with the horse!" I knew Macartney would kill him in good earnest, if he came back and found him with a living tongue in his head. "Don't you trust anyone but me—or someone who comes and gives you twenty dollars," I added emphatically, just because that was the only absolutely unlikely event I could think of. "And even then, you stay here till you see me! Understand?"

He said he did; it was easy enough to creep out after dark and rob rabbit traps; he was doing it now. And from the greed a fortune of twenty dollars had lit in his wretched eyes, I knew he would go on doing it till I came back. Of what wildly unexpected use he was to be to me in his waiting, heaven knows I had no thought. I crept out of his burrow as I had crept in, got back to my half-frozen horse, and rode hell for leather back to the Halfway. And just there was where I slumped.

My horse had to be fed and rested; he was dead beat when I led him into the unlocked stable, and when I had seen to him I meant to rouse up Billy Jones and tell him all the ugly stuff I had unearthed—and seen too—for the killing of four innocent men was hot in my mind. But I did not, for the excellent reason that Billy was not back. His house was dark, and his four horses still away from their vacant stalls. I sat down on a heap of clean straw to wait for him, and I said I slumped. I went sound, dead asleep. If I was hunting for excuses I might say it was two in the morning, and I had been up most of the night before. But anyhow, I did it. And I sat up, dazed, to see a lantern held in front of my eyes and one of Macartney's men from La Chance staring at me.

It struck me even then that it was not he who was surprised; and the sleep jerked out of me like wine out of a glass. "What are you doing here? And where the devil's Billy?" I snapped, without thinking.

I saw the man grin. "Billy's fired," he returned coolly. "Him and his wife got it in a note from Wilbraham, day before yesterday, when your teamsters stopped here on their way to Caraquet. They doubled up their teams with Billy's and took him and his wife along, and all their stuff. And I guess they'd been fired too, for they ain't come back. Mr. Macartney sent me over to see. Anything I can do for you?"

"Take that lantern out of my eyes, and hustle me up some breakfast. I— I'm sorry about Billy!" I was not; I was startled—and worse. It had not been Dudley who had dismissed him, asinine as he had been about Billy and old Thompson, or he would have told me. It had been Macartney, getting rid of him and my teamsters under my very nose; and—as Macartney's parting grin recurred to me—if his man had anyone with him in Billy's vacant shack they had been put there to get rid of *me*.

"Get me a bucket of water and make coffee, if you haven't done it," I said, yawning. "I'll come in—as soon as I've fed my horse."

But I did neither. I stopped yawning, too. Through the frosty window, as the man disappeared for the shack, I saw a light in its doorway and two more of Macartney's men standing in it, black between the lamp and the gray morning glimmer. I stirred some meal into the water Macartney's man had brought, drank a mouthful before I let my horse have just enough to rinse his throat with, and threw on his saddle. It was flat on his neck that I came out the stable door, and what Macartney's men meant to have done I don't know, for I was down the road toward La Chance like a rocket. And before I had made a mile I knew I had got off none too soon, for we were going to have snow at last, and have it hard.

Before I cleared the corduroy road it cut my face in fine stinging flakes, and by the time I was halfway to La Chance it was blinding me. It came on a wind, too, and I cursed it as I faced it, with my horse toiling through the heavy, sandy stuff that was too cold and dry to pack. The twenty-two miles home took me most of the day. It was close on dusk when I fumbled through drifting, hissing snow and choking wind, to the door of the La Chance stable. And the second I got inside I knew Macartney's man had told the truth, and Macartney had fired my teamsters with Billy Jones. There was not a soul about the place, and ten hungry horses yelled at me at once as I stamped my half-frozen feet on the floor. I would have shouted for Charliet if it had not seemed quicker to feed them myself. I yanked down a forkful of hay for each of them, after I saw to my own horse. And if you think I was a fool to worry over dumb beasts, just that small delay made a difference in my immediate future that likely saved my life. If I had raced off for the house at once I might have met with— Well, an accident! But that comes in later.

As it was I was a good twenty minutes in that stable. When I waded out into the swirling white dusk of snow and wind between me and the shack I was just cautious enough, after the Halfway business, to stare hard through the blinding storm at the house I was making for, though I did not think Macartney was ripe to dare anything open against me at La Chance. But with that stare I knew abruptly that he was! Massed just inside the open door of Dudley's shack, that was black dark but for one light in the living-room window, were a crowd of men that looked like nothing in the world but our own miners, that I knew now for Hutton's—or Macartney's—gang! How he dared have them there, instead of in the bunk house, beat me—but it was them, all right. The wind was clear of snow for one second, and I saw them plainly. And they saw me. Without one sound the whole gang jumped for me. I had my gun out, and I could have stopped the leaders before I had to get back against the stable door; but there was no need.

There was a shout behind me. The men checked, sprawling over each other in the snow—ludicrously, if I had been seeing much humor in things— and it was then it struck me that I should have had an accident if I had bolted straight into a dark house, instead of delaying in the stable till Macartney's gang got tired of waiting for me and bundled out themselves to see where I was. But I only wheeled, with my gun in my fist, to Macartney's voice.

What I had expected to see I don't know. What I did see, stumbling through the drifts to me, was an indistinguishable figure that turned out to be two. For it was Macartney, carrying Marcia Wilbraham. And behind him, short-skirted to her knees, and with no coat but her miserable little blue sweater, came my dream girl.

I forgot Macartney could not know I knew he was Hutton, or all the rest that I did know. I said, "What hell's trick are you up to now?"

But Macartney only turned a played-out face to me. "Take her from me, will you?" he snapped. "I'm done." He let Marcia slip down into the snow. "Wilbraham's killed!"

# CHAPTER 14

## WOLVES—AND DUDLEY

It was cleverly done. So was the desperate gesture of Macartney's hand across his blood-shot, congested eyes. If I had not had Thompson's deuce of hearts in my pocket I might have doubted if Macartney really were Hutton, or had had any hand in the long tale of tragedy at La Chance. But as it was I knew, in my inside soul, bleakly, that if Dudley were dead Macartney had killed him—as only luck had kept him from killing me.

I saw him give a quick, flicking sign to his men with the fingers of the hand that still covered his eyes, and I knew I was right in the last thing, anyhow, for the men straggled back from us, as to an order. They were to do nothing now, before Paulette and Marcia, if their first instructions had been to ambush inside the shack to dispose of me when I got back from the Half-way—which I had not been meant to do. I did not drop my gun hand, or fling the truth at Macartney. But I made no move to pick up Marcia. I said, "How d'ye mean Dudley's killed? Who killed him?"

"Wolves!" If Macartney meant me to think he was too sick to answer properly he was not, for he spoke suddenly to the bunk-house men. "There is no good in your waiting round, or looking any more. They've got Mr. Wilbraham, and"—he turned his head to me again—"they damn nearly got me!"

Later, I wished sincerely that they had, for it would have saved me some trouble. At that minute all I wanted was to get even with Macartney myself. I said, "Pick up Marcia and get into the house. You can talk there!"

Macartney glanced at me. Secretly, perhaps, neither of us wanted to give the other a chance by stooping for a heavy girl; I knew I was not going to do it. But Paulette must have feared I was. She sprang past me and lifted Marcia with smooth, effortless strength, as if she were nothing.

Macartney started, as though he realized he had been a fool not to have done it himself, and wheeled to walk into the house before us, where he could have slipped cartridges into his gun; I knew afterwards that it was empty. But Paulette had moved off with Marcia and a peremptory gesture of her back-flung head that kept Macartney behind her. I came behind him. And because he had no idea of all I knew about him, he took things as they looked on the surface. With Paulette leading, and me on Macartney's heels, we filed into the living room. There was a light there, but the fire was out. I guessed Charliet was hiding under his bed—in which I wronged him. But I was not worrying about Charliet or cold rooms then. Paulette laid Marcia down on the floor, and I stood in the doorway. I did not believe the bunk-house men would come back till an open row suited Macartney's book, but there was no harm in commanding the outside doors of the shack, all the same. And the sudden thought that we were all in the living room but Dudley, and that he would never come back to it, gripped my soul between fury and anguish. "Get it out—about Dudley," I said; and I did not care if my voice were thick.

Macartney looked over at me just as an honest, capable superintendent ought to have looked. "I can't; because I don't know it. All I do know's this. After you went off yesterday Wilbraham got to drinking; the wolves began to howl round the place after dark, and he said they drove him mad. He got a gun and went out after them—and he never came back. I didn't even know he was gone till midnight. I thought he'd shut himself in his office as he often does, till I heard shots outside, and found he wasn't in the house. I turned out the bunk-house men to look for him that instant, and when the lot you saw waiting in the shack for me came home toward morning, and said they couldn't find a sign of Wilbraham, and the bush was so full of wolves they were scared to go on looking, I went myself—"

"And took *girls*"—I remembered the reek of my wolf-doped clothes till I fancied I could smell the stuff there in the room, thought of a half drunk man walking out on a like baited track, and two girls taken over it to look for him—"into bush like that!"

"They followed me," curtly. "I didn't know it till it was too late to turn them back! I couldn't have sent Miss Wilbraham back, anyhow; she was nearly crazy. And if you're thinking of wolves, it was getting daylight, and—" he hesitated, and I could have filled in the pause for myself, remembering how that wolf dope acted: two lambs could have moved in the bush with safety, so long as they kept away from where it was smeared on the ground. But Macartney filled it in differently. "And, anyhow, it was well they did come. It was Marcia—found Wilbraham!"

I don't think I had really believed Dudley was dead till then. I stared at Marcia, lying on the floor as purple in the face from over-exertion and fright as if she had had an apoplectic fit, and at Paulette stooping over her, silent, and white around the mouth. She looked up at me, and her eyes gave me fierce warning, if I had needed it.

"Marcia got afraid and bolted for home—the wrong way," she spoke up sharply. "When I ran after her she was standing in some spruces, screaming and pointing in front of her. I saw the blood on the ground, and— Here's Dudley's cap! I found it, all chewed, close by." She pulled out a rag of fur from under her snow-caked sweater; and as the stale reek of the Skunk's Misery wolf dope rose from the thing, I knew the smell in the room had been no fancy, and how Dudley Wilbraham had died. I wheeled and saw Macartney's face—the face of a man who took me for a fool whose nose would tell him nothing.

"D'ye mean *that* was all you found?" I got out.

"No! The rest was there. But it was—unrecognizable! Even I couldn't look at it. It was—pretty tough, for girls. I shot one wolf we scared off it, but I couldn't do anything more. I couldn't lift—it; but—Dudley's coat was on it." He had turned so white that I remembered his faint in the assay office, like you do remember things that don't matter. I would have thought him chicken-hearted for a wholesale murderer, if it had not been for the cold hate in his eyes.

"D'ye mean you left Dudley—out there in the bush? Where the devil was Baker, that black and white weasel you set to look after him? I'll bet he saved *his* skin! Where is he?"

"Baker's missing, too," simply; and I did not believe it. "And I don't see what else I could have done but leave Dudley. None of the men were with me to carry him in; it had begun to snow; and in another hour I couldn't have kept the track back to La Chance. As it was, Miss Marcia played out; I had to carry her most of the way. And that's all there is to it," with sudden impatience, "except that Wilbraham's dead and Baker's missing. If he wasn't, he would have brought Dudley in."

"Yes," I said. I saw Charliet's head poke around the corner of the kitchen door and called to him to carry Marcia to her room, and to get fires going and something to eat; for the oddest part of it was that there seemed to be two of me, and one of them was thinking it was starving. It saw Charliet and my dream girl take Marcia out, and the other me turned on Macartney.

"By gad, there's one thing more," I said slowly. "You don't have to go on playing moving pictures, Dick Hutton, or using an alias either! You've killed Dudley and Thompson, and for a good guess Dunn and Collins, if I can't be sure—and you'd have had me first of all, if your boulder and your wolf dope hadn't failed you on the Caraquet road!"

Macartney's furious, surprised oath was real. "I don't know what you mean! Who on earth"—but he stammered on it—"Who d'ye mean by Hutton?"

"You," said I. "And if you're not he, I don't know why! There's no one else who would have followed Paulette Valenka out here. I don't believe what you've done's been all revenge on the girl you tried to get into trouble about Van Ruyne's emeralds, or scare that Dudley would worm out the truth about that, either: but if it was to jump the La Chance mine too, you're busted! Your accident serial story won't go down. I knew about your wolf dope business long ago, and do you suppose *this*," I shoved Dudley's cap under his nose, "doesn't tell me how you limed the trap you set for Dudley last night, or what you smeared on his clothes when he was too drunk to smell it? I know what brought the wolves to howl around this house, if I don't know how you shoved Dudley out to them. I know it was a home-made raid you had down at the assay office, and—I've been to Skunk's Misery!"

"Well?" said Macartney thickly.

"Well enough! I have Thompson's deuce of hearts you didn't see was missing, when you gave me back his pack! With any luck I'll pay you out for that, and our four mill men, *and* Dudley; not here, where you can fight and die quick, but outside—where they've things like gallows! Oh, you would, would you?"

For his empty gun just missed me as he made a lightning jump to bring it down on my head, and my left hand stopped him up just under the ear. I ought to have shot him. I don't know why I held back. I was so mad with rage when he dropped that I could have jumped on him like a lumberman and tramped the heart out of him. But I only lit for the kitchen, and Charliet's clothesline. As I got back and knelt down by the man who had called himself Macartney, Thompson rose up before me, as he had sat in that very room, playing his lonely solitaire; and the four dead men in the assay office; and Dudley—only I had no grief for Dudley, because it was drowned in rage. I bound Macartney round and round with the clothesline, whether he was really Hutton or not—and I meant to have the truth out of him about that and everything else before I was done. But when I had him gagged with kitchen towels while he was still knocked out, I sat back on my heels to think; and I damned myself up and down because I had not shot Macartney out of hand.

I had Macartney all right; but I had next door to nothing else, unless I could find a safe place to jail him while I disposed of his men. Now, if they chose to rush me, I could not hold the eight shack windows against them, if Paulette and I might each hold a door. If I took to the bush with Paulette and Marcia, *and* Macartney, I had nowhere on earth to go. There could be no piling that ill-assorted company on horses and putting out for Caraquet, with the road choked with snow, even if I could have got by Macartney's garrison at the Halfway. Crossing Lac Tremblant, that by tomorrow would be lying sweetly level under a treacherous scum of lolly and drifted snow, ready to drown us all like Thompson—I cursed and put that out of the question. That lake that was no lake offered about as good a thoroughfare as rats get in a rain-barrel. Whereas, to hold Macartney at La Chance till I downed his gang—

"By gad," I flashed out, "I can do it—in Thompson's abandoned stope!" It was not so crazy as it sounds. Thompson's measly entrance tunnel would only admit one man at a time, and I could hold it alone till doomsday. Macartney could be safely jailed inside the stope till I had wiped out his men;

Paulette would be safe; and there remained no doubtful quantities but Marcia and Charliet the cook. I guessed I could scare Marcia and that Charliet would probably be on my side, anyway. If he were and sneaked down now to provision the stope, the thing would be dead easy, even to firewood, for Thompson had yanked in a couple of loads of mine props and left them there. I lit out into the passage to hunt Charliet and find out where the bunk-house men had gone to. But there was no sign of either in the wind and snow outside the shack. I bolted the door on the storm, turned for the kitchen, and saw my dream girl standing outside Marcia's room.

She was dead white in the dim candlelight that shone through Marcia's half-open door. I thought of that as I jumped to her, and I would have done better to have thought of Marcia. I could see her from the passage, lying on her bed, purple-faced still, and with her eyes shut. But one glance was all I gave to Marcia. I said:

"For heaven's sake, Paulette, don't look like that! I'm top-sides with Macartney now. Got him tied up. Come into the kitchen till I speak to you. I want Charliet—" But as I pushed Paulette before me, into the kitchen just across the passage from Marcia's room, I stopped speaking. She was holding out Thompson's case of cards—open, with that scrawled two of hearts on the top!

"Charliet's gone—run away somewhere." Her chest labored as if she were making herself go on breathing, "and you dropped—this! I ran out from Marcia to see what you were doing with Macartney," she hesitated on the name, "and you'd dropped this. I— You know Macartney killed Dudley, really. Does this mean he killed *Thompson*, too?"

"You can say Macartney's real name," I snapped bitterly. "I've known he was Dick Hutton ever since last night."

But Paulette only gasped, as if she did not care whether I knew it or not, "Where—how—did you get these cards?"

I told her, and she gave a low moan. "Dudley's dead, and I'm past crying." Her voice never rose when she was moved; it went down, to D below the line on a violin. "I'm past everything, but wishing I was dead, too, for I'm the reason that brought Dick Hutton here as Macartney. Oh, you should have let me meet him that night! I wasn't only going to meet him; I meant to go away with him before morning. It would have been too late for poor, innocent old Thompson, but it would have saved the four mill men—and Dudley!" She had said she was past crying, but her voice thrilled through me worse than tears; and it might have thrilled Marcia in her room across the passage, if I'd remembered Marcia. "God knows Dudley was good to me— but it's no use talking of that now. What have you done with Macart—with Dick Hutton—that you said you had him safe for now?"

"Knocked him out; and tied him up with the clothesline, in the living room—till I can take him out to Caraquet to be hanged!"

"You ought to have killed him," Paulette answered very slowly. "I would have, when we found Dudley, only he'd taken my gun. At least, I believe he had: he said I'd lost it. And I'm afraid, without it—while Dick Hutton's alive!"

I looked at her ghastly face and behaved like a fool for the hundredth time in this history; for I shoved my own gun into her hand and told her to keep it, that I'd get another. I would have caught her in my arms if it had not been for remembering Dudley, who was dead because the two of us had held our tongues to him. "Look here," I said irrelevantly. "D'ye know Marcia thinks Macartney wants to marry her?"

"He doesn't want to marry anyone—except me," Paulette retorted scornfully; and once more I should have remembered Marcia across the passage, only I didn't. "He's made love to Marcia, of course, for a blind, like he did everything else. If we could make her realize that and that he killed Dudley as surely as if he'd lifted his own hand to him—"

But I cut her off. "By gad, Paulette, what sticks me is what Macartney did all this *for*!"

"Me," said Paulette very bitterly. "At least, at first; I'm not so sure about it now. When I first met Dick we were in Russia. He'd got into trouble over a copper mine—you've heard Macartney talk of the Urals?"—if we both spoke of him as though he were two different men neither of us noticed. "He came to me in Petrograd, penniless, and I helped him. But when I came to America, alone, I turned him out of my flat. He may have loved me, I don't know; but when I wouldn't marry him, he said he'd make me; that he'd hound me wherever I went and disgrace me, till I had to give in and come to him. And he *must* have done it at the Houstons', if I don't know how; for the police would take me now for those emeralds I never stole, if they knew where I was. I can't see where Dick could have been or how he managed the thing, but all the rest Dudley told you and him about that night at the Houstons' was true. I did give Van Ruyne sleeping stuff to keep him quiet while I got away, but it was because it came over me—the second I knew those emeralds were gone—that Dick must be in that house!—that if I didn't run away, he'd come in and threaten me till I had to go with him. And I'd have died first. I slipped out of the house unseen; and it was just the Blessed Virgin," simply, "who made me find Dudley's car stalled outside the Houstons' gate!"

"D'ye mean you'd known Dudley before?"

She nodded. "I'd met him: and I liked him, because he never made love to me. He hadn't been at the Houstons' that night; he was only coming back from Southampton alone, without any chauffeur. I knew no one would ever think he'd helped me, so I just got into his car. But I never should have let him bring me here," bitterly; "I should have known Dick would find me, and play gold robberies here to pay Dudley out. He told me he would, unless I'd go away with him—that first night you heard me talking to him—but I didn't see how he could work it. I thought I could tire him out by always balking him—till that night I didn't meet him, and he killed those four men. Then I knew I couldn't fight him; and the reason was that Dick's a finished mining engineer who never ran straight in his life!"

"What?" I knew both things, only I saw no connection with Paulette.

But she nodded. "He could get good work anywhere, but he won't work honestly. All he cares for is the excitement of big things he can get at crookedly. That was why he tried a *coup* with that copper mine in the Urals and had to clear out of Russia. And the La Chance mine that he came to contemptuously, and just to get hold of me, is a big thing too. No—listen! You don't know how big, for you've been kept in the dark. But Dick knows; and that's how I first knew I couldn't manage him any more, and why I don't think it is I he has done all he has for, nor that it was even to pay out Dudley. I believe it was to *get the mine*!"

"Then why, in heaven's name, didn't you tell Dudley who he was?"

"I couldn't make Dudley listen, at first. Then," very low, "I didn't dare; I knew it would mean that Dudley would get killed. I never thought that—would happen, anyway."

"There was me." I was stung unbearably. "You must have known ever since the night I first came here that there was always me!"

"Y-you," she stumbled oddly on it. "I couldn't tell *you*! Can't you see I was afraid, Nicky, that you might—get killed for me, too?"

For the first time that night she looked at me as if she saw me—me, Nicky Stretton, dark, fierce and dirty—and not Dudley Wilbraham and the dead. My name in that voice of hers would have caught me at my heart, if I had dared to be thinking of her. But I was not. It had flashed through me that Marcia's door had been half open when we went into the kitchen—and that now it was shut!

It was a trifling thing to make my heart turn over; but it did. I covered the passage in two jumps to the living-room door. But as I flung it open, all I had time to see was that the window was open too; with Marcia standing by it in her horrible green shooting clothes, just as she had lain on her bed, and a crowd of bunk-house men swarming through the open sash behind her and Macartney—Macartney, standing on his feet without any clothesline, with his gun in his hand!

I saw, like you do see things, how it had all happened. I had misjudged Macartney's intellect about the bunk-house men; he had had them within call. But it was no one but Marcia who had let them in, and she had freed Macartney. She had overheard Paulette and me in the kitchen, had shut her door, slipped out of her own window and into the living room, and cut Macartney's rope. She had no earthly reason to connect him with Dudley's death, except the scraps of conversation she had overheard from Paulette and me; she knew nothing of the bottle of wolf dope that had been meant to smash in my wagon, or that Dudley—so full up with drink and drugs that he could not have smelled even that mixture of skunks and sulphide—could easily have been sent out reeking with it, into bush that reeked of it too. And that second she screamed at me: "You lie, Nicky Stretton; you, and that girl! He's not Hutton—he's Macartney!"

But Macartney fired full in my face.

It was Marcia's flying jump that made him miss me. Even though his very cartridge was one of hers that she always carried in her pockets, and must have been given to him the first thing, I don't think she had been prepared to see me killed. I didn't wait to see. I was down the passage to Paulette before Macartney could get in a second shot. As he, and some of the bunkhouse men tore out of the living room after me, I fired into the brown mass of them with my own gun, that I snatched from Paulette. I thought it checked them, and lit out of the kitchen door, into the wind and the dark and the raving, swirling snow, with my dream girl's hand gripped in mine. We plunged knee-deep, waist-deep through the drifts, for our lives—for mine, anyhow.

"Thompson's stope," I gasped; and she said yes. I couldn't see an inch before me, but I think we would have made it, since Macartney could not see, either. I knew we were far ahead of him, but that was all I did know, till I heard myself shout to Paulette, "*Run!*"—and felt my legs double under me. If something hit me on the head like a ton of brick I had no sense of what had happened, as people have in books. I only realized I had been knocked out when I felt myself coming to. Somehow it felt quite natural to be deadly faint and sick, and lying flat, like a log—till I put out my hand and touched hard rock.

"I don't see how it's rock," I thought dully; "it ought to be snow! Something hit me—out in the snow with Paulette!" And with that sense came back to me, like a red-hot iron in my brain. I *had* been out in the snow with Paulette; one of Macartney's men must have hit me a swipe on the head and got her from me. But—where in heaven's name was Paulette now? The awful, sickening thought made me so wild that I scrambled to my knees to find out in what ungodly hole I had been put myself. I had been carried somewhere, and the rock under me felt like the mine. But somehow the darkness round me did not smell like a mine, where men worked every day. It smelt cold, desolate, abandoned, like—

And suddenly I knew where Macartney's men had carried me when I was knocked out! It was no comfort to me that it was to the very place where

I had meant to jail Macartney and hide Paulette, where Charliet and I were to have stood off Macartney's men.

"Thompson's stope," I gasped. "It's there Macartney's put me!" I crawled, sick and dizzy, to what ought to have been the tunnel and the tunnel entrance, opening on the storm out of doors. The tunnel was there, all right. But as I fumbled to what ought to have been the open entrance, stillness met me, instead of a rush of wind; piled rock met my groping hands, instead of piled snow. I was in Thompson's abandoned stope all right—only Macartney had sealed up the only way I could ever get out! I shoved, and dug, and battered, as uselessly as a rat in a trap, and suddenly knew that was just what I was! Macartney had not even taken the trouble to kill me—not to avoid visible murder at this stage of the game, when only the enemy was left, if you did not count a duped woman and a captured one; but for the sheer pleasure of realizing the long, slow death that must get me in the end.

"Die here—I've got to die here," I heard my own voice in my ears. "While— My God, Paulette! Macartney's got Paulette!"

And in the darkness behind me somebody slipped on a stone.

I had not thought I could ever feel light and fierce again. I was both, as I swung round.

# CHAPTER 15

## THE PLACE OF DEPARTED SPIRITS

Every man carries his skull under his face, but
God alone knows the marks on it.
                    —Indian Proverb.

For a man moved, silent and furtive, in the tunnel between me and the stope!

At the knowledge something flared up in me that had been pretty well burnt out: and that was Hope. That anyone was in the place showed Macartney had either put a guard on me—which meant Thompson's abandoned stope was not sealed so mighty securely as I thought—or else it was he himself facing me in the dark, and I might get even with him yet. I let out a string of curses at him on the chance. There was not one single thing he had done—to me, Paulette, or anyone else—that I did not put a name to. And I trusted Macartney, or any man he had left in the ink-dark stope, would be fool enough to jump at me for what I said.

But no one jumped. And out of the graveyard blackness in front of me came a muffled chuckle!

It rooted me stone still, and I dare swear it would have you. For the chuckle was Dunn's: Dunn's—who was dead and buried, and Collins with him! But suddenly I was blazing angry, for the chuckle came again, and—dead man's or not—it was mocking! I jumped to it and caught a live throat, hard. But before I could choke the breath out of it a voice that was not Dunn's shouted at me: "Hold your horses, for any sake, Stretton! It's us."

A match rasped, flared in my eyes, and I saw Dunn and Collins! Saw Dunn's stubbly fair hair, clipped close till it stood on end, as it had on the skull I'd said a prayer over and buried; saw Collins standing on the long shank bones I knew I had buried in the bush!

I stared, dazed, facing the two boys I could have sworn were dead and buried. And instead Dunn gasped wheezingly from the rock where I had let him drop, and Collins drawled as if we had met yesterday:

"We heard we were dead! But it wasn't us you buried, or any of Hutton's men either, for he'd have missed 'em. I expect you'd better put your funeral down to two stray prospectors, and let it go at that!" He looked curiously into my face. "You don't seem to have got much yourself by playing the giddy goat with Hutton!"

In the dying flicker of his match I saw his young, sneering eyes, as he called Macartney "Hutton," and realized furiously that Paulette had been right, not only that Dunn and Collins were alive, but that they were on Macartney's side. I blazed out at the two of them:

"So you've been in with Hutton all along, you young swine! I've been a blank fool; I ought to have guessed Hutton had bought you!"

Dunn let out a sharp oath, but Collins only threw down the glowing end of his match. "I wouldn't say we were on Hutton's pay roll exactly, since you seem to have found out Macartney's real name at last," he retorted scornfully. "We've been on our own, ever since we saw fit to disappear and bunk in here. Though by luck Hutton hasn't guessed it, or we wouldn't be here now!"

"I don't know that it's any too clear why you are here," I flung out hotly. "D'ye mean to say you've been living here, *hiding*, ever since you cleared out, and I thought the wolves ate you? That you knew all along who Macartney was—and never told me?"

"Not exactly here, if you mean Thompson's old stope you're corked up in; but of course we knew Macartney was Hutton," Collins returned categorically. "As for telling you about him—well, we weren't any too sure you weren't Hutton's man yourself—till tonight!"

"*What?*" said I.

But Collins apologized calmly. "We were asses, of course; but we couldn't tell we'd made a mistake. We didn't have as much fun as a bag of monkeys while we were making it, either, especially when there was that—trouble—in the assay office. We came in on the tail-end of that, only we'd no guns, and it was too late to help our poor chaps, anyway. Besides, we thought you—" but he checked abruptly. "It's too long to explain in this freezing hole. Let's get out! You're not corked up here so dead tight as Hutton-Macartney thinks," and in the dark I knew he grinned. "Only I imagine we'd better decide what we're going to do before he discovers that!"

"Do? I've got to get Paulette!" But I lurched as I turned back to the blocked tunnel entrance, and Collins caught me by the shoulder.

"You can't get her," said he succinctly, "unless we help you! Going to trust us?"

It didn't seem to me that I had any choice; so I said yes. Then I gaped like a fool. Dunn and Collins had me by the arms and were marching me through the dark, not toward the tunnel where I'd been slung in, but back through Thompson's black, abandoned stope, as if it had been Broadway, till the side wall of it brought us up. "Over you go," said Collins gruffly. He gave me a boost against the smooth wall of the stope, and my clawing fingers caught on the edge of a sharp shelf of stone. I swung myself up on it, mechanically, and felt my feet go through the solid stope wall, into space. There was an opening in the living rock, and as Collins lit another match where he stood below me, I saw it: a practicable manhole, slanting down behind my shelf so sharply that it must have been invisible from Thompson's stope, even in candlelight. Collins and Dunn swarmed up beside me, and the next second we all three slid through the black slit behind our ledge, and out—somewhere else. Collins lit a candle-end, and I saw we were in a second tunnel, a remarkably amateur, unsafe tunnel, too, if I'd been worrying about trifles, but not Thompson's!

The thing made me start, and Collins grinned. "More convenient exit than old Thompson's, only we don't live here! If you'll come on you'll see." He and his candle disappeared round a loose looking boulder into a dark hole in the tunnel side, and his voice continued blandly as I stumbled after. "Natural cave, this tunnel was, when we found it; this second cave leading out of it; and a passage from here to—outside!" He waved his hand around as I stood dumb. "Our little country home!"

What I saw was a small round cave, the glow of a fire under a shaft that led all betraying smoke heaven knew where into the side of the hill, and two spruce beds with blankets. The permanent look of the place was the last straw on my own blind idiocy of never suspecting Macartney, and I burst out, "Why the deuce, with all you knew, couldn't you have brought Paulette here and hidden her?"

"Charliet said we should have." Collins nodded when I stared. "Oh, yes, there's more to that French Canadian than just cook! He's been in the know about us here all this time, or we'd have been in a nice hole for grub. Mind, I don't say he's brave—"

"He was under his bed when I wanted him tonight," I agreed with some bitterness.

"Was he?" Collins exclaimed electrically. "He was here, giving us the office about you! He tore down and told us you'd got Hutton, and we'd better light out and help you: but when we turned out it looked more as if Hutton had got *you*! When you and Miss Paulette rushed out of the kitchen door you must have run straight into an ambush of his men, and I guess one of them landed you a swipe on the head. Anyhow, Dunn and I met a procession with you frog-marched in the middle of it, that was more than we could manage without guns. So we kind of retired and let the men cork you into Thompson's stope to die. And you bet they did it. Not six of us could have got you out, ever, if we hadn't known a private way."

I cursed him. "My God, stop *talking*! It's not me I want to hear about. Where was Paulette? D'ye mean you followed me and left her—left a girl—to Macartney? I—I've got to go for her!"

But Collins caught me as I turned. "Macartney hadn't got her—she wasn't there! We hoofed Charliet off to find her, first thing; he'll bring her here, as soon as it's safe to make a getaway. We'd have brought her ourselves, only the show would have been spoiled if Hutton had spotted us. And we had to hustle, too, to get back here and waltz you out of Thompson's mausoleum. It'll be time enough for you to go for Miss Paulette when she doesn't turn up. You're not fit now, anyway." I felt him staring into my face. "Had anything to eat all day, except a hard ride and a fight?" he demanded irrelevantly, in a voice that sounded oddly far off.

I shook my head; and the smell of coffee smote my famished nostrils as he took a tin pot off the fire. I knew how nearly I had been done when the scalding stuff picked me up like brandy. But—"You're sure about Paulette?" I gasped. "Remember, Macartney was bound to get her!"

"Well, he didn't," Collins returned composedly. "I bet he's looking for her right now, and I'm dead sure he won't find her. Charliet wasn't born yesterday: he'll bring her here all right."

"I'll wait ten minutes," I gave in abruptly, and because I knew I couldn't do anything else till I had filled my empty stomach. But there was something I wanted to know. "What did you mean, just now, about not being sure of me—with Hutton?"

Dunn spoke up for the first time. "It was Miss Paulette; we thought it was you we heard her talking to, two nights in the dark. So when she drove off to Caraquet with you and the gold, after we'd heard her say she couldn't trust you—at least, the man we thought was you—we didn't know whether you were in with Hutton or not, or what kind of a game you were playing."

"Me?" I swore blankly. "I suppose it never struck you that *I* believed the man playing the game was Collins—till you both disappeared, and I decided it must be someone who never was employed around this mine!"

"Well, I'm hanged," said Collins, and suddenly knocked the wits out of me by muttering that at least we'd both had sense enough to know that Miss Valenka was square.

"Valenka? D'ye mean you knew who she was, too?" I stuttered.

"Dunn did," Collins nodded. "I only knew Hutton. But I knew more than my prayers about him, and Dunn told me about the girl. So we sort of kept guard for her and watched you and Hutton—till the day we had the row with him."

"In the mine! He told me." Only half of me heard him. The rest was listening for the sound of footsteps. But the place was still.

"In Thompson's stope," Collins corrected drily. "You see, we thought you and Macartney-Hutton were working together, and we didn't see our way to tackling the two of you at once. So when you went off to Caraquet with Miss Paulette, we thought we'd get Hutton cleared out of this before you got back again. We kind of let him see us leave work in the mine and sneak into the old stope. When he came after us, we dropped on him with what we knew about him; and between us we knew a deal. We gave him his choice about leaving the neighborhood that minute, or our going straight to Wilbraham and telling who he was and what he was there for—which was where we slipped up! He'd the gall to tell us to our faces that we'd no pull over him, because we were doing private work in Thompson's stope and stealing Wilbraham's gold out of it. And—that rather gave us the check."

"But—why? There wasn't six cents' worth of gold there to steal!"

Collins smiled with shameless simplicity. "I know. But stealing gold was exactly what we were doing, only it wasn't in Thompson's old stope. We'd have been caught with the goods on us though, if anyone had fussed round there to investigate. We found our way in here," he jerked his head toward his amateur tunnel, "by accident, in Thompson's time, one day when the stope happened to be empty; and we burrowed on to what looked like the anticlinal, before we heard the stope shift coming and had to slide out. But we'd seen enough to keep us burrowing. We couldn't do much, even after Hutton ran the other tunnel half a mile down the cliff and caught gold there; but we kind of slipped in, evenings, when you missed us out of the bunk house"—he grinned again—"and got the bearings of that vein. And you bet we had to find a way to stay with it; it was too good to leave! We weren't going to work in Wilbraham's mine just for our health and days' wages, when we'd struck our own gold. So we reckoned we'd just—disappear. But we didn't get out as sharp as we did simply on account of our own private affairs. Macartney-Hutton drew a gun the day we had the row he lied to you about, and I guess we just legged it out of Thompson's stope—by the front way!—in time to make the bush with our lives on us. Macartney thought he'd scared us, and we'd lit for Caraquet; but we lit back again after dark. We crawled in here by our back entrance you haven't seen yet, and here we've been ever since! We didn't confide in you, because you seemed pretty thick with Macartney, if you come to think of it; and it seemed a hefty kind of a lie, too, when you told Charliet you'd buried us. I rather think that's all, till tonight—" his indifferent drawl stopped as if it were cut off with a knife. "My God, Stretton," he jerked, "I'd forgotten! Was it true—what Charliet told us tonight—about Dudley Wilbraham?"

I was eating stuff the silent Dunn had supplied, but I put the meat down. "Wilbraham's killed," I heard my own voice say; and then told the rest of it. How Paulette had found Dudley's chewed, wolf-doped cap, and Marcia had found Dudley, silent in the silent bush, where the last wolf was sneaking away. I would not have known Collins's face as he asked what I meant about wolf dope now and when I thought I was swearing at Macartney in Thompson's stope.

I told him, with my ears straining for Charliet and a girl creeping to us, through Collins's back way out. But all I heard was silence—that thick, underground silence that fills the ears like wool. I had said I would wait ten minutes, and nine of them were gone. I don't think I spoke. Dunn muttered suddenly, "They're not coming!"

Collins shook his head and coldly cursed himself and me for two fools who had lain low, when out in the open together we could have stopped Macartney from getting Dudley, if we couldn't have helped old Thompson. He never mentioned Paulette, or his trusted cook. But he rose, lit a second candle, and led the way out of his warm burrow by a dark hole opposite the one we had entered by, and into a cramped alley where we had to walk bent double. It felt as if it ran a mile before it turned in a sharp right angle. Collins pinched out his light and turned on me. "Just what—are you going to do?"

"Get Paulette," said I.

"M-m," said Collins. "Well, here's where we start. Get hold of my heels when I lie down and don't crowd me." And that was every word that came out of either of us as we dropped flat, and wormed head-first down a slope of smooth stone till cold, fresh air abruptly smote my face. In front of us was an opening, out of the bowels of the hill, into the night and the snow. Rooted juniper hung down over it in an impervious curtain, as it hung everywhere from the rocks at La Chance. Collins pushed it aside, and the two of us were out—out of Thompson's stope, where Macartney had meant me to lie till I died!

# CHAPTER 16

## IN COLLINS'S CARE

For two breaths I did not know where I was. It was still snowing, and the night was wild, such a night as we might not have again for weeks. Any one could move in it as securely as behind a curtain, for I could not see a yard before my face, and not a track could lie five minutes. But suddenly the familiarity of the place hit me, till I could have laughed out, if I had been there on any other business. Collins's long passage had wormed behind Thompson's stope, behind the La Chance stables; and it was no wonder he had found it easy enough to get supplies from Charliet. All he had to do was to cross the clearing from the jutting rock that shielded his private entrance and walk into Charliet's kitchen door. I moved toward it, and Collins grabbed at me through the smothering snow.

"Hang on—you don't know who's there! Wait till I ring up Charliet, number one Wolf!" He stood back from me, and far, far off, with a perfect illusion of distance broken by the wind, I heard a wolf howl, once, and then twice again. If he had not stood beside me, I could not have believed the cry came from Collins's throat. But, remembering Dudley, it had an ill-omened sound to me.

"Shut up!" I breathed sharply.

Collins might have remembered Dudley too. "I wasn't going to do it again," he muttered, "but I've had to use it for a signal. It's been a fashionable kind of a sound around here, if I hadn't sense enough to know Macartney brought the beasts that made it. But Charliet knows my howl. He'll come out, if he's— Drop, *quick*!"

But both of us had dropped already. Some one had flung open the kitchen door and fired a charge of buckshot out into the night. I heard it scatter over my head, and a burst of uproar on its heels told me Charliet's kitchen was crowded with Macartney's men. Somebody—not Charliet—shouted over the noise, "What the devil's that for?" And another voice yelled something about wolves and firing to scare them.

"The boss'll scare you—if you get to firing guns this night," the first voice swore; and a man laughed, insolently. Then the kitchen door banged, and Collins sprang up electrically.

"I don't like this one bit," he muttered. "Macartney's not in the house, or his men wouldn't dare be yelling like that; and Charliet's not there, either, or he'd have been out. That devil must have got him somewhere—him and Miss Paulette! Can't you see there's not a light in the shack, bar the kitchen one? Come on!"

But I was gone already, around the corner of the shack to Paulette's side of it, and I knew better. There was a light—in Paulette's room—shining through a hole in the heavy wooden shutters she had had made for her window, long before I guessed why she wanted them and their bars. It ran through me like fire that Macartney was in that room, deaf to any kind of yells from the kitchen, to everything but Paulette's voice; and nobody but a man who has had to think it can guess what that thought was like to me, out there in the snow. I made for my own window, but it was locked; and God knew who might be watching me out of it, as I had watched Macartney one night, before I knew he was Hutton. I thought: "By gad, Nick Stretton, you'll go in the front door!" For that—with me shut up to die in Thompson's stope, and not one other soul alive to interfere with him—was the last thing Macartney would think to lock! Nor had he. The latch lifted just as usual, and I walked in.

The long passage through the shack was dark; and, after the storm outside, dead silent. It was empty, too, as the living room was empty; but what I thought of was my dream girl's door. That was open a foot-wide space, and somebody inside it sobbed sickeningly. But if Macartney were there he was not speaking. I daresay I forgot I had no gun to kill him with. I crept forward in the soundless moccasins I had reason to thank heaven were my only wear and suddenly felt Collins beside me, in his stocking feet.

"Hang on," he breathed; "I tell you he isn't there! If he were, you couldn't get him. One shout, and he'd have the whole gang out on us!"

I knew afterwards that he'd stubbed his toe on Marcia Wilbraham's little revolver she'd dropped on the passage floor, and was ready to keep my back if the gang did come; but then I hardly heard him. I stood rooted at Paulette's door, staring in; for Paulette was not there—Macartney was not there! What I saw was Marcia Wilbraham with her back to me, crying hysterically, as I might have known Paulette would never cry, and flinging out of a trunk, as if Paulette were dead or gone, every poor little bit of clothes and oddments that were my dream girl's own!

I can't write what that made me feel. Ribbons, bits of laces, little blue stockings, shoes, grew into a heap. And I would have been fool enough to jump in on Marcia and shake out of her how she dared to touch them, whether Paulette were dead or alive, if Collins had not gripped me hard.

"The emeralds," he muttered. "She's rooting for them!"

I had pretty well forgotten there ever were any emeralds, and I stared at him like a fool.

"Van Ruyne's emeralds—she thinks Miss Paulette has 'em," Collins's lips explained soundlessly. "And they're round Macartney's own neck—I saw them! Dunn and I were going to swipe them, only we couldn't."

I damned the emeralds. What I wanted of Marcia was to find out what had become of Paulette. But Collins gripped me harder. "Let her see you, and you'll never know," he breathed fiercely. "She'd give one yell, and we'd be done. Macartney's either got the girl and Charliet, or they're lost in the snow and he's hunting for them. Let's get some guns and go see which; we're crazy to stay here!"

I nodded mechanically. I knew what it meant for a girl to be lost in the snow on such a night as I had just closed the shack door on, even with Charliet beside her; how Collins and I might tramp, search—yes, and call, too—uselessly, beside the very drift where she lay smothered. And then I realized I was a fool. Macartney would not give Paulette a chance to get lost. He had her somewhere, her and Charliet, and Collins and I had to take her from him. But something inexplicable stopped me dead as I turned for the shack door. Macartney had never been a winter at La Chance; he had no snowshoes. Charliet had some, I didn't know where. But I had two pairs in my own room. That inexplicable suggestion told me I needed them badly, though I knew it was silly; if Macartney had Paulette he would not be marching her through the snow. All the places I had to search for her were the stable and the assay office. And yet— I backed Collins noiselessly past the room where Marcia was still pulling round Paulette's trunk, with a noise that covered any we could make, and the two of us ended up in my room in the black dark. I stood Collins at the door while I felt for my snowshoes. I knew it was crazy, and I was just obsessed, but I got them. I didn't get much else. I couldn't find my rifle I had hoped for, and only a couple of boxes of revolver cartridges were in my open trunk—that I guessed Marcia had gone through too. I would have felt like wringing her neck, if it had not been for Paulette and Macartney. I had no room for outside emotions till I knew about those two. I slid back to my doorway to get Collins, and he was gone. Where to, I had no earthly idea. I looked to see if he had been cracked enough to tackle Marcia, and Marcia was alone on her knees, chucking all Paulette's things back into her trunk again. The place suddenly felt dead quiet. Marcia had stopped sobbing, and I believe she would have heard a mouse move—there was that kind of a listening look about her. And it was that minute—that unsuitable, inimical minute—that I heard someone move! Outside, on the doorstep, somebody stumbled. The latch lifted, the door swung in—and I jumped to meet Macartney with not one thing on me but some fool snowshoes and a pocketful of useless cartridges. But I brought up dead still, and rigid.

"Charliet—oh, Charliet, come *quick*," whispered Paulette. She was snow from head to foot where she stood in the shack door. "I couldn't find—" But she recoiled as she saw me, against the light Marcia had burning inside her own half-open door. "Oh, my God, *Nicky!*" she cried in a voice that brought my soul alive, that fool's soul that had lost her. She caught at me like a child, incredulously, wildly. "Oh, Nicky!"

There was no time to ask where she'd been, nor even of Macartney. I think the unsuitable thing I said was "Marcia!" For I heard Marcia jump and fall over Paulette's open trunk, before she was out of her door like one of the wolves Macartney was so fond of. I didn't think she saw us, but she did see Collins. The thing that cut her off was his rush out of somewhere. I heard her scream with furious terror; heard Paulette's door bang on her; and Collins was beside me with a rifle and some dunnage I scarcely saw in the sudden dark of the passage after that banged door.

"Run," said he, through his teeth. "Gimme that stuff! Run!" he stuffed my snowshoes under the arm that held the rifle. "No, not that way! This way." He cut across the clearing in the opposite direction from the hole that led to his underground den, and it was time. Half of Macartney's men were tearing through the passage toward Marcia's screams, and the rest were pouring out of the kitchen door. In the storm we could only hear them. I was carrying Paulette like a baby, and with her head against me I could not see her face. All I could see was swirling, stinging snow in my eyes, and the sudden dark of the bush we brought up in. I kept along the edge of it, circling the clearing, and all but fell over the end of Collins's jutting rock. And this time I thanked God for the furious snow; in ten minutes there would be no sign of our tracks from the front door to the hold the rock shielded, and there was no earthly chance of Macartney's men picking them up before we were safe.

It felt like years before the three of us were inside the curtain of juniper, swarming up the smooth rock face, but Collins observed contrarily that he'd never done it so quickly. He led the way up to the passage angle where he had pinched out his light, put down the snowshoes and the rifle, laid something else on the ground with remarkable caution, and walked on some feet before he lit his candle.

"Better travel light and get home. Dunn and I'll come back presently and bring up the dunnage," he observed as blandly as if the three of us had been for an evening stroll, and suddenly laughed as he saw me glance at his stockinged feet. "By golly, I've left my boots in the shack, and I haven't any others—but it was worth a pair of boots! I stubbed my toe on Miss Wilbraham's little revolver she must have dropped on the passage floor, and I've got it. Also, let alone her lost toy-dog gun, I got all her ammunition and her rifle, while she was grabbing in Miss Paulette's trunk."

*" 'Taffy went to my house,*
*Thought I was asleep.*
*I went to Taffy's house,*
*And stole a side of beef'*

—as I learned when I was young. Come on, Stretton; I bet we'll be top-sides with Macartney-Hutton yet!"

"He's out, looking for me—" but Paulette's sentence broke in a gasp. "Why, it's Collins!" She stared incredulously in the candlelight.

"Just that," imperturbably. "Stretton can tell you all about me presently, Miss Paulette. For now I imagine you'd sooner see a fire and something to eat. Put her in between us, Stretton, Indian file, and we'll take her down."

Women are peculiar things. Tatiana Paulina Valenka had tramped the bush most of the day before looking for a dead man, had found him—a sight no girl should have looked on; had run for more than her life with me, and been through God knew what since; and she walked down that unknown, dark passage with Collins and me as if nothing had ever happened to her. She greeted Dunn, too; and then, as he and Collins disappeared to fetch down our snowshoes and rifle, went straight to pieces where she and I stood safe by their fire. "Oh, oh, oh, I thought you were dead! I saw them get you. I can't believe—can't believe—" she gasped out in jerks, as if she fought for her very breath, and suddenly dropped flat on Dunn's old blanket. "Oh, Nicky," she moaned, "don't let me faint—now. *Nicky!*"

There was something in her voice—I don't know—but it made me dizzy with sheer, clear joy. She had said my name as if I were the one man in the world for her, as if I had risen from the dead. But I dared not say so. I knew better than even to lift her head where she lay with closed eyes on Dunn's blanket, but I got Collins's old tin cup to her lips somehow and made her drink his strong coffee till it set her blood running, as it had set mine. After a minute she sat up dizzily, but she pushed away my bread and meat. "Presently—I'd be sick now," she whispered. "How did you get—out of Thompson's stope? And where—I mean I can't understand, about Collins and Dunn!"

"They got me out," said I, and explained about them. But there was no particular surprise on Paulette's face. She never made an earthly comment, either, when I told her they'd always known all about her and Hutton, except, "I never thought they were dead; I told you that. I'd an idea, too, that Charliet didn't think so either."

I had one arm round her by that time, feeding her with my other hand like a child, with bits of bread soaked in black coffee. If I had any thoughts they were only fear that she might move from me as soon as she really came to herself. But Charliet's name brought me back from what was next door to heaven. "Charliet," said I blankly; "where in the world is he? D'ye mean he hadn't told you about Collins and Dunn? Why, he was to bring you to them—here—hours ago!"

"Charliet was? But—" Suddenly, beyond belief, my dream girl turned and clung to me. God knows I knelt like a statue. I was afraid to stir. It was Dudley she loved: I was only a man who was trusted and a friend. "Oh, Nicky, you don't know," she cried, "you don't know! You and I ran straight *into* some of Dick Hutton's men when we raced out of the shack. And you threw me—just picked me up like a puppy and threw me—out of their way, into the deep snow. I heard them get you, but I was half smothered; I couldn't either see or speak. But I heard Dick shout from somewhere to 'chuck Stretton into Thompson's old stope!' I thought it meant they'd killed you; that it was another man I'd let—be murdered!"

She caught her breath as if something stabbed her, and I know it stabbed me to think I was just "another man" to her. But I knelt steady. I had been a fool to think it was I she cared for, personally, and whether she did or not she needed my arm. "Well?" I asked. "Next?"

"I was scrambling out of the snow," I felt her shiver against me, "only before I could stand up Charliet raced up from somewhere and shoved me straight down in the drift again. He said Dick was looking for me, and to lie still, while he got him away; then to race for the shack and hide just outside the front door, till he came for me—but before he could finish Dick ran down on the two of us, with a lantern. He'd have fallen over me, if Charliet hadn't stopped him by yelling that I'd run for the bush. I think he grabbed the lantern—but anyhow, they both tore off. I got to the shack, but— Oh, Nicky, I couldn't wait there. I—"

"Well?" It seemed to be the only word in my brain.

"I went down to Thompson's stope. But I was too late. The men had walled you in with rocks, and I couldn't move them. I tried!" (I thought she must hear the leap my heart gave. I know I shut my jaws to keep my tongue between my teeth at the thought of her trying to dig her way in to me, the only friend she had in the world except a French-Canadian cook.) "I— Oh, I thought if I could find Charliet we might do something! I went back to look for him, and I found *you*— Oh, I found you!" Her arms were still on my shoulders as I knelt by her, and suddenly her voice turned low and anxious. "What do you suppose became of Charliet? He's so faithful. We can't leave him for Dick to turn on when he can't find me!"

I was not thinking of Charliet. I couldn't honestly care what had become of him, with my dream girl in my arms. I may as well tell the truth; I forgot Dudley, too. I don't know what mad words would have come out of my mouth if Paulette had not pushed me away violently. What was left of her coffee upset; I got to my feet with the empty cup in my hand, just as Collins and Dunn and their candle emerged round the boulder. I remembered long afterwards that it was before I had answered Paulette one word about myself, Thompson's stope, anything. But then all I did was to stare at something Collins was carrying carefully in his two hands. "What's that?" I said—just to say something.

"Some new kind of high explosive Wilbraham got to try and never did," Collins returned casually. "Saw it in his office tonight and thought it was better with us than with Macartney. Don't know just how it works, so I'm treating it gingerly." He moved on into the darkness of his own tunnel and came back empty-handed. "What are we going to do—first?" he inquired calmly.

I took a look at Paulette. Whether it was from Collins's casual mention of Dudley's name or not, she was ghastly. Who she was looking at I don't know; but it wasn't at me.

"Sleep," said I grimly. "Two of us need it, if you and Dunn don't. Macartney can't get us tonight." Though of that I was none too sure. Charliet might get rattled any moment and give us away. But there was no good in sticking at trifles.

But Collins was an astute devil. "He won't," he rejoined as calmly as if I had spoken of Charliet out loud. "He won't get hurt, either; you can bank on that. Make up that fire, Dunn, and we'll give Miss Paulette the blankets."

We did, where she lay at one side. We three men dropped like dogs in a row in front of the fire. I was next Paulette, with the space of a foot or so between us. I had not known how dead weary I was till I stretched out flat. Collins and Dunn may have slept; I don't know; but Paulette certainly did, as soon as she got her head down. I thought I lay and watched the fire, but I must have slept, too. For I woke—with my heart drumming as if I'd heard the trump for the Last Judgment, and Paulette's hand in mine. I must have flung out my arm till I touched her, and her little fingers were tight round my hard, dirty hand, clinging to it. I lay in heaven, in the dark of a frowsy cave we might be hunted out of any minute, with the dying glow of the fire in my eyes and my dream girl's hand in mine. And suddenly, like a blow, I heard her whisper in her sleep, "Dudley! Oh, dear Dudley!"

I was only Nicky Stretton, and a fool. I lay in the dark with a heart like a stone and a girl's warm, clinging hand in mine.

# CHAPTER 17

## HIGH EXPLOSIVE

There was nothing to tell of any handclasp when I woke in the morning. Paulette lay in her blankets with her back to me, as if she had lain so all night; Dunn was making up the fire; Collins was absent, till he appeared out of his tunnel where he had put Dudley's high explosive the night before and nodded to me. None of us spoke: we all had that chilly sort of stiffness you get after sleeping with your clothes on. As we ate our breakfast I took one glance at Paulette and looked away again. She was absolutely white, almost stunned looking, and her eyes would not meet mine. I had an intuition she had waked in the night after I slept and discovered what she had been doing; but if she were ashamed there was no need. God knows I would not have reminded her of the thing. I knew the dark hollows and the tear marks under her eyes were for Dudley, not for me. But I had to take care of her now, and Collins glanced at me as I thought it.

"I suppose you realize Charliet's our only line of communication, and that he and all the La Chance guns are in the hands of the enemy," he observed drily. "What do you think of doing about it?"

"Get Charliet; all the guns and ammunition he can steal; hold this place and harry Macartney," I supposed. "What do *you* think?"

I had turned to Paulette, but she only shook her head with an, "I don't know, Mr. Stretton!" I had time to decide she had only called me Nicky by mistake six hours ago, before Collins disagreed with me flatly.

"Stay here? Not much! Won't work—Macartney'd drop on us! Oh, I know he won't be able to find our real entrance to this place unless Charliet gives us away, and I'm not worrying about that! But, after he realizes Miss Valenka has vanished"—he said her real name perfectly casually—"and when Charliet and most of his guns vanish too, and his men begin to get picked off one by one, how long do you suppose it will be before Macartney connects the three things—and smells a rat? He'll sense Charliet and a girl can't be fighting him alone. For all we know he'll guess you must have got out of Thompson's stope somehow, and dig away his rock fence to see! And I imagine we'd look well in here if he did!"

"It's just what we would look," said I. "You ass, Collins, with Macartney ignorant of the real way in on us, and he and his gang digging open Thompson's tunnel against the daylight, with you and me and Dunn in the dark on that shelf in Thompson's stope we came in here by, we'd have the drop on the lot. Except—Marcia!" Her name jerked out of me. We would have to count Marcia in with Macartney's gang; and, remembering she had known me all her life, it made me smart.

"Oh, Miss Wilbraham—I should let *her* rip!" Collins returned callously. "Listen, Stretton; what you say's all very well, only we can't count on holding this place when we're discovered, while it's a matter of *if* Charliet can get guns! Miss Marcia's rifle and her toy popgun aren't going to save us, and I doubt if Charliet can swipe any more. What I say is let's cut some horses out of the stable after dark, all four of us clear out on them to Caraquet, and set the sheriff and his men after Macartney. Unless," he turned boldly to her, "you don't want that, Miss Valenka?"

But if she had been going to answer, which I don't think she was, I cut her off. "We can't let Marcia rip—don't talk nonsense, Collins! She's Dudley's sister, if she and Macartney are a firm. We can't clear out and leave her with a man like that!"

"We can't take her to Caraquet," Collins argued with some point. "You own she doesn't know anything about Macartney's wolf dope; you haven't any witnesses to prove he tried it on your wagon, or to set the wolves on Dudley. Miss Marcia would just up and swear your whole story was a lie— and all Caraquet would believe her! Nobody alive ever heard of such a thing as wolf dope!"

"That's just where you're wrong!" I remembered the boy I'd left cached in Skunk's Misery—and something else, that had been in my head ever since wolves and the smell of a Skunk's Misery bottle seemed to go together. "Two Frenchmen were run in for using wolf dope in Quebec province last winter, for I've an account of their trial somewhere that I cut out of an Ottawa paper. And as for a witness, I've a boy cached at Skunk's Misery who can prove Macartney made the same stuff there. The only thing we might get stuck on in Caraquet is the *reason* for all the murders he's done—with, and without it!"

"I guess Miss Valenka knows the reason all right," Collins spoke as coolly as if she were not there, which may have been the wisest thing to do, for though she flushed sharply she said nothing. He went on with exactly what she had said herself. "But after Hutton came here to get her, he saw he'd be a fool not to grab the La Chance mine, too; and unless we can stop him you bet he and his gang have grabbed it! They've disposed of Thompson, of all our own men who might have stood by us, of Wilbraham," categorically; "they think they've disposed of Dunn and me and buried you alive, and—except for having lost Miss Valenka—Macartney's made his game! Nobody'll know there's anything wrong at the mine till the spring, because there's no one interested enough to ask questions till Wilbraham's bank payments have stopped long enough to look unusual. And by that time Macartney and his gang will be gone and the cream of Wilbraham's gold with them. As for us, we can't fight him by sitting in this burrow *with* Miss Paulette, and without any guns, even if he doesn't end by nosing out Dunn's and my gold as well as Wilbraham's. Why, we depend on Charliet for our food, let alone anything else; and for all we know, Charliet may have squeaked on us by this time. I say again, let's get a sheriff and posse at Caraquet, and come back here and get Macartney! We could do it, if we took Miss Paulette and hit the trail tonight."

"And Macartney'd get us, if we tried it!" I had thrashed all that out in my head before, while I was tying up Macartney with Charliet's clothesline. "We'd be stopped by his picket at the Halfway, if ever we got to the Halfway, for the Caraquet road's likely drifted solid and you don't make time digging out smothering horses. No; we'll fight Macartney where we are! And the way to do it is with Charliet and guns."

"If you'll tell me how we're to connect with either!" Collins was grim. "It's a mighty dangerous thing calling up Charliet on number one Wolf, with the whole of La Chance crawling with Macartney and his gang, hunting for Miss Paulette. But we can go up to the back door and try it!"

"Oh, no," Paulette burst out wildly, "I'm afraid! I mean I know we must find out first if Charliet's all right, but you mayn't get him—and you'll give yourselves away!"

It was almost the first time she had spoken, and it was more to Collins than to me, but I answered. "We'll get Charliet all right," I began—and Collins gripped me.

"I dunno," he drawled. "Strikes me someone's going to get us—first!"

He snapped out our candle, which was senseless, since Dunn's red-hot fire showed us up as plain as day, and all four of us stood paralyzed. Somebody—running, slipping, with a hideous clatter of stones—was coming down the long passage Collins called his back door.

"Macartney," said I, "and Charliet's given us away!" And with the words in my mouth I had Paulette around the waist and shoved out of sight behind the boulder that separated Collins's cave from his tunnel and the pierced wall of Thompson's stope. Macartney might be a devil, but there was no doubt the man was brave to come like that for a girl, through the dark bowels of the earth where Charliet must have warned him Dunn and Collins would be lurking. Only he had not got Paulette yet, and he would find three men to face before he even saw her. I stooped over her in the dark of Collins's tunnel, where just a knife-edge of the cave firelight cut over the boulder's top. "Keep still,

Paulette—and for any sake don't move and kick Collins's devilish explosive he's got stuck in here somewhere," I said, exactly as if I were steady. Which I was not, because it was my unlooked for, heaven-sent chance to get square with Macartney. I sprang around the boulder to do it and saw Collins strike up the barrel of Marcia's rifle in Dunn's stretched left arm.

"Don't shoot," he yelled. "You fool, it's Charliet!"

I stood dead still. It was Charliet, but a Charliet I had never seen. His French-Canadian face was tallow white, as he tore into the cave, grinning like a dog with rage and excitement. He brushed Dunn and Collins aside like flies and grabbed my arm. "Come out," he panted. "Sacré damn, bring Mademoiselle Paulette and *come out*! It is that Marcia! She sees you in the shack last night; sees you—alive and out of Thompson's stope where they buried you—carrying Mademoiselle away! She tells Macartney so this morning, when he and I get in after hunting for Mademoiselle all night—praying, me, that I might not make a mistake and find her, and that you might. Oh, I tell you I was crazy—dog crazy! I cannot get away from Macartney, I think she may be dead in the snow, looking for me who was not there, till first thing this morning we come in—and that she-devil tells Macartney Stretton takes Mademoiselle away! Not till now, till all are out of the house, do I have the chance to come and warn you what is coming! They—that Marcia, Macartney, all of the men—start now to dig you out of Thompson's stope they put you in. They think they left some hole you crawl out of in the snow and dark, that you come for Mademoiselle and take her back into. I could not get you even one small cartridge to hold this place, and—Macartney is clever! He will be in here, with all his guns, all his men. And then, *quoi faire*? Come now, all of you, while there is the one chance to come unseen, and get on horses and go away. Ah," the man's fierce voice broke, ran up imploringly, "I beg you, Mademoiselle, like I would beg the Blessed Virgin, to make them come! Before Macartney, or that Marcia, finds—you!"

I jumped around and saw Paulette, in the cave. I had left her safe in Collins's tunnel; and there she stood, come out into plain view at the sound of Charliet's voice. But she was not looking at him, or me, or any of us. Her eyes stared, sword-blue, at the hole where Charliet had rushed in from Collins's secret passage: I think all I realized of her face was her eyes. I turned, galvanized, to what she stared at—and saw. Marcia Wilbraham was standing in the entrance from the long passage, behind us all, except Paulette; meeting Paulette's eyes with her small, bright brown ones, her lips wide in her ugly, gum-showing smile. I knew, of course, that she had picked up Charliet's track in the snow from his kitchen door to Collins's juniper-covered back door, had followed fair on his heels down the dark passage, instead of going with Macartney to dig me out of Thompson's stope; that in one second she would turn and run back again, to show Macartney Collins's back door.

My jump was late. It was Dunn who saved us. He sprang matter-of-fact-ly, like a blood-hound, and pulled Marcia down. She was as strong as a man, pretty nearly; she fought fiercely, till she heard the boy laugh. That cowed her, in some strange way. I heard Dunn say: "You'd better stay here a while, Miss Wilbraham. It's safer—than with Macartney." I saw Charliet run to help him, and the two of them placidly tied and gagged Marcia Wilbraham with anything they could take off themselves. It was with a vivid impression of Charliet's none too clean neck-handkerchief playing a large part in Marcia's toilette that Collins and I jumped, with one accord, to Paulette. I don't know what he said to her. I saw her nod.

I said, "We're done for if Macartney gets in on us through Thompson's stope and finds this place. He'll just send half his men to scout for the other entrance; they'll find it from Charliet's and Marcia's tracks and get at us both ways. You stay here with Charliet, while Collins and I meet Macartney in Thompson's stope. When—if—you hear we can't best him, run—with Charliet! Dunn'll look after Marcia."

She gave me a stunned sort of look, as if I were deserting her, as if I didn't care! I would have snatched her in my arms and kissed her, Dudley or no Dudley lying dead in the bush, but I had no time. Collins had me by the elbow, his fierce drawl close to my half-comprehending ear. We'd no guns but Marcia's popgun and her rifle; two of us, even on the shelf in Thompson's stope, would do little good with those against all Macartney's men crowding into the stope and giving us a volley the second our fire from the shelf drew theirs. We might pick off half a dozen of them before our cartridges gave out. But there was no sense in that business. We would have to try— But here I came alive to what Collins was really talking about.

"That high explosive," he was saying. "It's a filthy trick, but God knows they deserve it! If we blow them back far enough at the very entrance of the tunnel, they may never come on again to get in."

I daresay I'd have recoiled in cold blood. But my blood ran hot that morning. I did think, though; hard. I said, "Can't do it! No fuse."

"Heaps. Dunn's and mine!" I heard Collins grabbling for it, somewhere in the dark of the tunnel.

Behind me somebody lit a candle; who, I never looked to see. In the light of it I saw Collins pick up his bundle of blasting powder and warned him sharply.

"Look out with that stuff! We don't know it; it may work anyway. If it bursts up in the air the stope roof'll be down on us. It may fire back, too—and we'd be hit behind the point of burst!"

"We won't be," said Collins, between his teeth. "I'll burst it *out* the tunnel, and blow Macartney's gang to rags!"

But that lighted candle at my back had shown me other than explosives: the silly, pointless snowshoes I had lugged from my own room in the shack. My conscious mind knew now what my subconscious mind had wanted them for, like a mill where someone had turned on the current. I swore out loud. "By gad, Collins, listen! If we don't smash Macartney, and he gets in on us, he'll get Paulette! I've got to stop that, somehow. Macartney doesn't *know* she's here yet; Marcia only guessed it. Supposing he were to see only me, alone in Thompson's stope, he might never know she was here too!"

"Dunno what you mean," Collins snapped. And I snapped back:

"I mean that if we blow a clean hole at the tunnel entrance, and I burst out of it and run, I can get the whole gang after me—and make time for you and Charliet to get Paulette away somewhere, by the back door."

"But"—Collins halted where he swarmed up into Thompson's stope— "where'll you go? You can't, Stretton. It's death!"

"It's sense," said I. "As for where I'll go, Lac Tremblant'll do for me; and I bet it will finish any man of Macartney's who tries to come after me! Get through into that stope with your fuse, man; I'll hand you the blasting stuff. Got it? All right. Here you, gimme that candle!" I turned and took it— out of Paulette's hand!

I gasped, taken aback all standing, before I lied, "It's all right, Paulette. I'll be back in a minute." And though I knew she must have heard what I was going to do, I had no better sense than to stoop before the girl's blank eyes and snatch up my two pairs of snowshoes, that had been lying beside the explosive I had just passed up to Collins, before I clambered up through the hole into Thompson's stope, on to the shelf from whence I had first dropped into Collins's cave.

Collins was down in Thompson's tunnel already, laying his fuse with deadly skill. Already, too, we could hear Macartney's men outside, lever-aging away the boulders that had plugged up the tunnel entrance where I was to starve and die. Collins placed the stuff I carried down to him. I said, "My God, you can't use all that; the whole stope'll be down on us!" And he answered, "No; I've done it right." That was every word we uttered till we were back on our high shelf, with a lit fuse left behind us in the stope. The fuse burned smooth as a dream, and Collins nudged me with fierce satisfaction. But I was suddenly sick with horror. Not at the thing we were doing—if it were devil's work we had been driven to be devils—but at the knowledge that Paulette was standing within reach of my feet, that were through the stope wall and were hanging down into Collins's tunnel—that tunnel every bone in me knew was amateur, unsafe, a death trap. The shock of a big explosion in Thompson's stope might well bring its roof down on Paulette, standing alone in it, waiting—trusting to me for safety. I turned my head and yelled at her as a man yells at a dog—or his dearest—when he is sick with fear for her: "Get back out of that into the cave! *Run!*"

I heard her jump. Heard her— But thought stopped in me, with one unwritable, life-checking shock. The whole earth, the very globe, seemed to have blown to pieces around me. The flash and roar were like a thousand howitzers in my very face; the solid rock shelf I was on leapt under me; and behind me the whole of Collins's tunnel collapsed, with a grinding roar. I heard Collins gasp, "Good glory"; heard the rocks and gravel in the stope before me settling, with an indescribable, threatening noise, between thunder and breaking china—and all I thought of was that I'd warned my dream girl in time, that she'd answered me, that she was back in Collins's cave, and safe. Till, suddenly to eyes that had been too dazzled and seared to see it clearing, the smoke before me cleared, the choking fumes lessened, and I saw. Saw, straight in front of me, where a tunnel had been and was no longer, a clean hole like a barn door where Thompson's tunnel entrance had been but two-men wide; saw out, into furious, crimson color that turned slowly, as my sight grew normal, into the golden, dazzling glory of winter sun on snow.

There was silence outside in the sun, all but some yells and moaning. How much damage we'd done I couldn't see; or where Macartney's men were, dead or alive. But now, while they were paralyzed with shock and surprise, now was my time to get through them. I lowered myself gingerly to the rubbish heap that had been the smooth floor of Thompson's stope; edged to the tunnel entrance; slipped my feet into the toe and heel straps of the snowshoes I had held tightly against me through all the unspeakable, hellish uproar of rending rock, and sprang—sprang out into the sunlight, out on the clear snow, past wounded men, reeling men, dying men, and raced as I never put foot to ground before or since, for Lac Tremblant, glittering clear and free in front of me—that Lac Tremblant I had thought of subconsciously when I carried snowshoes into Collins's cave.

In the beginning of this story I said what Lac Tremblant was like. It was a lake that was no lake; that should have been our water-way out of the bush instead of miles of expensive road; and was no more practicable than a rope ladder to the stars. For the depth of Lac Tremblant, or its fairway, were two things no man might count on. It would fall in a night to shallows a child might wade through, among bristling rocks no one had ever guessed at; and rise in a morning to the tops of the spruce scrub on its banks—a sweet spread of water, with never a rock to be seen. What hidden spring fed it was a mystery. But in the bitterest winter it was never frozen further than to form surging masses of frazil ice that would neither let a canoe push through them, nor yet support the weight of a man. It was on that frazil ice, that some people called lolly, that I meant to run for my life now, trusting to the resistance of the two feet of snow that lay on the lake in the mysterious way snow does lie on lolly, and to the snowshoes on my feet. And as I slithered on to the soft snow of the lake, from the crackling, breaking shell ice on the La Chance shore, I knew I had done well. Some—a good many—of Macartney's men were killed or half-killed by our deadly blast, but not all. He had been more cautious than I guessed. I saw the rest of his men bunched some hundred feet from the smashed-out tunnel; saw Macartney, too, standing with them. But all I cared for was that he should see me and come out after me on the crust of snow and lolly over Lac Tremblant—that would never carry him without the snowshoes he did not have—and give Paulette her chance to get away. I yelled at him and skimmed out over the trembling ice like a bird.

Neither Macartney nor his men had stirred in that one flying glance I had dared take at them. But sheer tumult came out of them now. Then shots—shots that missed me, and a sudden howled order from Macartney I dared not turn my head or break my stride to understand. The giving surface under me was bearing, but a quarter-second's pause would have let me through. There was no sense in zigzagging. Once I was clear, I ran as straight as I dared for the other shore, five miles away; but—suddenly I realized I was not clear! I was followed.

Somebody else on snowshoes had shot out of Thompson's tunnel, over the crackling shore ice on to the snow and frazil; was up to me, close behind me.

"Run, Nicky," shrieked Paulette's voice. "*Run!*"

I slewed my head around and saw her, running behind me!

# CHAPTER 18

## LAC TREMBLANT

*"Across the ice that never froze*
*The snow that never bore,*
*My love ran out to follow me—*
*To follow to the shore."*
—The Day the World Went Mad.

It may be true that I swore aloud; but what I meant by it was more like praying. Over me was the blue winter sky and the gold sun; under me the treacherous spread of the lake that was no lake, that one misstep might send me through, to God knew what hideous depth of unfrozen water, or bare, bone-shattering stone; behind me were Macartney and Macartney's men; and close up to me, nearer every second, my Paulette, my dream girl who had never been mine. There was nothing to do for both of us but to keep on crossing Lac Tremblant. Missteps might be death, but turning back was worse—for her, anyway.

I yelled, "Keep wide! Get abreast of me—don't take any direction you don't see me take. But *keep wide!*" Because what held one of us would never hold two, and behind me, running in my tracks— Well, even a light girl would not run long!

Paulette only screamed, "Yes. Keep on! They're coming!" She may have needed her breath, I don't know; but she didn't run like it. She ran like a deer, with my own flat, heel-dragging stride on the snowshoes I had not thought she knew how to use. One more shot came after us. I yelled again to her to keep wide and heard her sheer off a little to obey me; but she still ran behind me. God knows I didn't realize, till afterwards, that it was to keep Macartney from shooting me. I didn't even wonder why Collins and Dunn weren't firing into the brown of Macartney's men with Marcia's rifle and popgun. I was too busy watching the snow surfaces before me.

There was a difference in them. I can't explain what, but a difference between where there was water to buoy the snow, and where it lay on shell ice. The open black holes where there was nothing at all anyone could see, and

I didn't worry over them. I only knew we must run over water, or the light stuff under us would let us through. I kept moving my hand in infinitesimal signals to Paulette, and God knows she was quick at understanding. My heart was in my mouth for her, but she never made a mistake, or a stumble where a stumble would have meant the end. She called to me suddenly; something that sounded like, "They're coming!"

I turned my head and saw out of the tail of my eye, as a man sees when he's riding a race. They *were* coming! Macartney's men, and—I thought—Macartney; but I knew better than to look long enough to make sure. His men, anyhow, had raced out on the lake as we had raced, and there was no need to watch what became of them. Their dying screams came to us, as they floundered and sank in their heavy boots through snow and frazil ice, to depths they would never get out of. I might have been sick anywhere else. I was fierce with joy out there in Lac Tremblant, running with a girl over the thin crust under which death lurked to snatch at us, as it had snatched at Macartney's men. Neither of us spoke. I was thinking too hard. I could have run indefinitely as we were running, but Paulette was just a girl. What of Paulette if she slackened with weariness, if I led her wrong by six inches, or missed a single threatening sign on the stuff we fled over?

If I had been sure Macartney was drowned with his men, I might have taken her back to La Chance; but I was not sure. And, Macartney or no Macartney, the track I had led her out on the lake by was the only one I would have dared trust to return on—and it was all lumps of snowy lolly and blue water, where Macartney's men had broken through. I looked ahead of me with my mind running like a mill. We had done about half the five-mile crossing; we might do the rest if we could stop and breathe for ten minutes, for five, even for two. Only, in all the width of the lake that lay like cake icing in front of us, there was not one place where we could dare to stand. The water under us was higher than I had ever known it. Not one single dagger-toothed rock showed as they had showed when I crossed it in a canoe the night before it froze to the thick slush that was all it ever froze to. There was not one single place to— But violently, out of the back of my memory, something came to me. There was one place in Lac Tremblant where, high water or low, a man might always stand—if I could hit it in the smothering, featureless snow.

"The island!" I gasped out loud. Because there was one—a high, narrow island without even a bush on it—rising gradually, not precipitately like the rest of the rocks in Lac Tremblant, out of the uncertain water. But for half an hour I thought it might as well be non-existent. Stare as I might I could see no sign of it—and suddenly I all but fell with blessed shock. I was on it; on the highest end of it, with solid ground under my feet; solid ground and safety, breath and rest. I yelled to Paulette, "Jump to me!" and she jumped. That was all there was to it, except a man and a girl, panting, staggering, clinging together, till sense came to them, and they dropped flat in the snow.

I said sense, but I don't know that I had any. I lay there staring at Paulette and her long bronze hair that had come down as she ran, till it was like a mantle over her and the snow round her. I had never thought women had hair like that. I cried out, "My God, Paulette, why did you come?"

I may have sounded angry. I was, as a man always is angry when he has dragged a woman into his danger. Paulette panted without looking at me. "I—had to! The tunnel—caved in!"

"I told you to get out of it!" I sat up where I had flung myself down and stared at her. She sat up, too, both of us crimson-faced and dishevelled. But neither of us thought of that. I stormed like a fool. "What possessed you to stay in the tunnel—or to follow me? I told you to jump for the cave!"

"Well, I didn't!" Paulette stiffened as if she froze. "I hadn't time. I would have had to cross the tunnel. And I hadn't *time* to do anything but jump to you and Collins before your stuff blew up. I'd just got on your shelf when it went off, and it stunned me till I had just sense enough left to lie still and hold on. But afterwards, when I saw what you were going to do, I put on the snowshoes you'd left by the tunnel entrance and came after you. I'm sorry I did, now!"

"But Collins—" I looked blankly across the two miles of quivering death trap we still had to cross before we gained what safety there might be in the Halfway shore and the neighborhood of Macartney's picket, and my thoughts were not of Collins—"Why, in heaven's name, didn't Collins have sense enough to lug you back into his cave with him and Charliet, instead of letting you take a chance like this?"

"Collins couldn't get back himself," Paulette retorted, as if I were unbearably stupid. "Nobody could get back! I told you the tunnel *caved in*, till it was solid between us and the others. Collins saw I had to follow you. In two more minutes Dick would have come to hunt Thompson's stope for me, and we had no guns to stave him off. You and Collins left them in the tunnel!" It was just what we had done, and I wasted good time in remembering it, guiltily. Paulette stood up and twisted back her streaming cloud of hair. "So, as I had to come with you," she resumed without looking at me, "don't you think we'd better get on? If you're waiting for me to rest, you needn't."

I wasn't, altogether. I stared back over the perilous way we had come. There was no black speck of anyone following us on its treacherous face; no sound of shots; no anything from the shore we had left. Yet, "Where do you suppose Macartney is?" I asked involuntarily.

"Dead." Her voice was almost indifferent, but she shivered. "Or he'd have gone on shooting at us."

I nodded, but I would have felt easier if I had thought so. Somehow I didn't, I don't know why. I know nothing would have induced me to take Paulette back to La Chance, even if the trodden lolly would have borne us again. I had a pang about Collins, left alone there; but Collins could take care of himself, and Paulette's shiver had reminded me we should freeze to death if we loitered where we were. I pointed to the snowy lake between us and the Halfway shore. "Can you do two more miles of running, over that?"

"Yes," she glanced down at her slim, trained body, rather superbly. "Only—there's no one following us! Have we got to be quite so quick?"

"Quicker! We don't know about Macartney. If he's alive he has a stable full of horses, and he knows where we're running to. He may try to cut us off." I half lied; he could not cut us off, since horses would be of no use to him in the heavy snow, and on foot it would take him two days to go round Lac Tremblant to the Halfway, where crossing the lolly could bring us in two hours. But I had no mind to air my real reason for haste.

I should have known Paulette was too shrewd for me. "I'm a fool—Lac Tremblant never bears, of course," she said quite quietly. "Go on, Mr. Stretton. Only—don't stop, if anything goes wrong with me!"

"Nothing will go wrong," said I, just as if I believed it. If she had called me Nicky, as she had done by mistake the night before, when she slept with her hand clasping mine, if she'd even looked at me, I must have burst out that I loved her, past life and death, and out to the world to come. But it was no time to force love-making on a girl who had seen the man she meant to marry lie dead before her eyes. If she turned shaky, or cried, I could never save her. For the bit of lake in front of us was ten times worse than what we'd crossed. I knew that when I tightened up the snowshoes silently and led my dream girl out on it. I would have given half my life for a rope, such as people have on glaciers. But I had no rope, and each of us would have to run, or sink, alone.

I meant, of course— But that's no matter. I got Paulette off the island and, inch by inch, feeling my way, back to the channel where buoyant water, at least, lay under us. I twisted and turned like a corkscrew, but I dared not leave it. Once I cautioned Paulette never to try a short cut, just to keep abreast of me; and twice my heart was in my mouth at a hollow, instant-long clatter under our shoes. But we got on over the stuff somehow, leaving holes of blue water in our tracks, with great gobbets of snow floating in them. The shore lay close in front of us, with a hard distinct edge of shell ice showing where the water stopped. I was just going to call out that in ten feet more we'd be safe over the lolly, when—smash—both of us went through! I thought I fell a mile before I hit the water that was going to drown us; hit it knees first, just as I'd gone through, and—I sprawled in icy slush that rose no higher than my waist. I was in a sort of pocket between two rocks that were holding up the lolly. There was an avalanche of caving snow and ice all round me, but I was not drowned or likely to be—only I barely thought of it. For I could not see Paulette. Suddenly, past belief, I heard her scream: "Nicky!"

I fought blindly to the sound of her voice, wormed between my screening rocks, and shouted as I stood up. She was not even in slush! She had gone through shell ice to bare ground, a long strip of bare ground that led straight to the Halfway shore; roofed, high above my head, with shell ice and lolly that filtered a silver-green light. My dream girl lay there in her little blue sweater with the wind knocked out of her—and that was all. I kicked off my snowshoes that were not even broken and carried her under the ice roof to the Halfway shore. I may have thanked God aloud; I don't know. Only I carried her, with my face close to hers, and the slush and snow from her falling over me as I stumbled under the ice roof to the blessed shore. I had just sense enough to drop her in the blinding daylight, and drop myself beside her. I couldn't speak, from dead cold fear, now that I had saved her, of what it would have been if I had not. For two gasping minutes we just lay there.

Then Paulette said pantingly, "I'm so dreadfully sorry—I've been such a trouble! But I couldn't do anything but come, and—I forgot you couldn't want me!"

I sat up and saw her, sitting on a cold, bare, wind-swept rock that was all the refuge I had to offer her. Half a mile farther on were food and shelter in the Halfway shack—and it might as well have been in Heaven, for with Macartney's men cached in it I naturally could not take her there. Behind that, twenty-seven miles off, was Caraquet; but even a girl with a trained body like Paulette's could never make twenty-seven miles on top of all we'd done.

"It's no question of wanting you," I exclaimed angrily. "It is that I don't know what to do. But want you—when do you suppose I haven't wanted you, ever since the night I first saw you by Dudley's fire? What do you suppose I'd ever have been in this game *for*, if I hadn't wanted just you in all this world? My heart of hearts, don't you know I love you?" I lost my head, or I never would have said it, for I saw her flinch. That brought me back to myself in the snow and desolation round us that stood for God's world as nothing else would have done. I burst out in shame, "Oh, forgive me! I never meant to let that out. I know you never cared a hang for me; that you were going to marry Dudley, if he hadn't been killed!"

For one solid minute Paulette never opened her mouth. She sat like a colored statue, with rose-crimson cheeks and gold-bronze hair, under the white January sun. Her eyes were so dark in her face that they looked like blue-black ink. "I—I never was engaged to Dudley," she gasped at last, more as if it were jerked out of her than voluntarily. "I didn't think it was any business of yours, but I never was. We—Dudley and I—only said so, because it seemed the simplest way to manage Marcia, when Dudley brought me here to get me out of that emerald business. He was good to me, if ever a man was good to a girl he was only sorry for; I can't forget that brought him to his death. I'm sick with sorrow for him—but I never was going to marry Dudley! He didn't even want me to. He— Oh, *Nicky*!"

Because I couldn't stand it; I'd seen her eyes. I had both her hands in mine, I think I was telling her over and over how I had always loved her, how I had stood out of Dudley's way, that I didn't expect, of course, that she could care about an Indian-faced fool like me, when—suddenly—I knew! Like roses and silver trumpets and shelter out there in the homeless snow, *I knew*! All Paulette said was, "Oh, Nicky," again. But the two of us were in each other's arms.

I don't know how long we clung or what we said. But at last I lifted my Indian-dark head from her gold one and spoke abruptly out of Paradise. "By gad, I have it!"

"Have what?" Paulette gasped. "Oh, you certainly have most of my hair; it's all wound up in your coat buttons—if you mean that!"

I didn't. "I meant I knew where we could go, and that's to Skunk's Misery," I harked back soberly, remembering the boy I had left there with a fire and shelter anyhow, if not food.

"But you said it was a horrible place!"

"So it is, when you have anywhere else to go. But we can't try the Halfway with Macartney's men in it, and neither of us could make Caraquet tonight. We've got to have shelter, darling."

Paulette stopped plaiting her hair in a thick rope. "Say that again," she ordered curiously.

"What—Skunk's Misery?" But suddenly I understood, and used that word I had never said aloud before:

"*Darling* darling, Skunk's Misery is our only chance. Get up and come on!"

But she answered without moving.

"Want to tell you something first. The tunnel falling in wasn't all the reason I ran after you. I thought—thought Dick might not dare to shoot at you if I were between you and him, so— Oh, Nicky, *don't* kiss my horrid, chapped hands!"

But I was glad to hide my humbled face on them, remembering how I had stormed at her. I muttered, "Why didn't you tell me—out there on the lake?"

"Well, you were pretty unpleasant, and"—as I kissed her, my dear love I had never thought to touch—"oh, Nicky, how could I tell you? I said everything to you last night but '*Nicholas Dane Stretton, I love you!*'—and all the notice you took was to kneel perfectly silent, with a face as long as your arm. You never even answered me, when I called you Nicky by mistake!"

I hadn't dared. But it was no time to be talking of those things. Let alone that my wet breeches had frozen till I felt as if my legs didn't belong to me, we had landed exactly where old Thompson had been drowned. I wanted to get away from there, quickly; leaving no more trail than was necessary. I looked round me and saw how to do it.

In front of us was the hole in the shore ice and all the smash and flurry where we had gone through. Where we had crawled on shore, from under the intact ice roof, was bare rock, wind-swept clean. It struck me that with a little management, and to a cursory inspector, it could look as though Paulette and I were drowned like Thompson. The snow had not piled on this side the lake as it had on ours. Detached rocks, few but practicable stepping-stones, lifted their bare bulk out of it, between us and the spruce bush we had to strike through to avoid the Halfway and Macartney's picket. Some kind of a trail we must leave to Skunk's Misery, but it need not begin here, in the first place Macartney would look, if he were alive to look anywhere. Paulette's eyes followed mine as I thought it, and she nodded. It was without a track of any sort, after the lake trail ended, that she and I stopped in the thick spruces and put on our snowshoes for the last lap of the way to Skunk's Misery.

My dream girl's trained young body served her well. As she stepped out after me, I would never have guessed she had run a yard. It was easy enough to avoid the Halfway, and unlikely that Macartney's men would ever discover our devious track in the thick bush. Crossing the Caraquet road was the only place where we had to leave a track in the open. I did the best I could with it by picking up Paulette, and carrying her and her shoes into thick bush again; but I could not honestly feel much pleasure in the result. Any one with any sense would know my sunken shoe marks had carried double, but it was the best I could do. It was no pleasure to me either to hear Paulette exclaim sharply, as I set her down:

"Nicky, I *forgot*! Dick can snowshoe after us, if he's alive. Charliet made a lot of snowshoes at odd times, to sell in Quebec if he ever went back there. They were piled up in the shed behind the kinty, and I believe Dick knew—though he didn't remember it in time to save his men. If he follows us I"—her lip curled in fear and hatred—"Oh, I hope he's dead!"

So did I. Yet somehow I had never felt it. "Well, if he isn't," I said roughly, "he'll have to do twenty-two miles to catch up to our five, and then some to Skunk's Misery. He couldn't make good enough time round the lake to catch us tonight, supposing he knew where we were going; even on the chance of him, we've got to have one night's rest. And our only place to find it is Skunk's Misery!"

Paulette nodded and stepped out after me once more. It was dead toil in the soft snow, and it was slow; for Macartney or no Macartney, there was no making time in the untrodden bush. I cut our way as short as I dared, but do the best I could it was dark when we came to that forlorn, evil hollow in the gap of desolate hills that Caraquet folk called Skunk's Misery. That had its points though, considering we needed to reach Macartney's old lean-to unseen, for the Skunk's Misery population was in bed, and as I said before, they had no dogs to bark at us. In dead silence, with Paulette holding to my coat and our snowshoes under our arms, we went Indian file through the maze of winding tracks Skunk's Misery used for roads, under rocks and around them; and on the hard-trodden paths our feet left no trace. At least, I thought so: and it was just where I slipped up! If I had looked behind me, when Paulette would not let me carry her snowshoes, I would have seen the tails of them dragging a telltale cut in the snow behind her, as they sagged from her tired arm. But my eyes were straight before me, on the door of Macartney's lean-to. It hung open, as it had always hung, but I only glanced in to make sure it was empty. It was elsewhere I was going, around the huge boulder that backed the place, and down a gully that apparently brought up against blind rock—only I knew better. I found the opening of the rocky passage I had wormed down once before with my back scraping the living rock between me and the sky, and on my hands and knees, with Paulette after me, I went down it again. It ended without warning, just as I had known it would end, in an open cave. A glow of fire was ahead of me; and, stooping over it—what I had never imagined I should see with joy and gratitude—the boy I had left there, toasting a raw rabbit on a stick. That was all I saw. And what possessed me I don't know, but as I stood up I turned on Paulette with a sudden wave of stale jealousy overwhelming me, and a question I had kept back all the afternoon:

"Paulette, you're sure—*sure*—it's me, and not Dudley? That you didn't love the poor chap best?"

Paulette scrambled to her feet beside me. "It's you," she said clearly. "I told you Dudley never loved me, or I him. I'll mourn for him always, for he met his death through me. But he never wanted to marry me, and if he were alive, he'd be the first person to tell you so!"

There was a pause, definite, distinct, while you could count five. The boy at the fire started to frozen attention at sight of us, as sharply as his distorted body could start. But before he could speak, or I did, another voice answered Paulette's from the dark of the cave behind the fire—an unexpected, mind-shattering voice, that took me toward it with one bound. "By gad," it said, "he would, would he? Two things have to go to that!"

I stood paralyzed where I had jumped. Paulette's snowshoes dropped clattering on the cave floor. Dudley Wilbraham, whom the wolves had eaten—little, fat, with a face more like an egg than ever, but whole and *alive*—stood in the dimness of the cave behind the fire and my Skunk's Misery boy!

# CHAPTER 19

## SKUNK'S MISERY

Paulette said, "Oh my heavens, Dudley!" and went straight to pieces.

I don't know that I made much of a job of being calm myself. All I could get out was, "The wolves! We thought they'd eaten you—Paulette found your cap out by the Caraquet road."

Dudley, for whom the whole of La Chance had beaten the bush all one livelong night, whom his own sister had sworn was killed and eaten, Dudley made the best show of the three. He had a flask, of course—when had he not? He dosed Paulette and me with what was left in it, but even with the whisky limbering my parched throat I hadn't sense to ask a coherent question. Dudley looked from Paulette to me and spoke pretty collectedly to both of us.

"I wasn't eaten, if that's what brought you two here—though judging from your conversation I imagine it wasn't. Thank the Lord you are here though, anyway. I've been pretty wild, tied up here with this snow. But"—sharply—"where the devil's Marcia?"

"Hidden away from Macartney, with Charliet to look after her." It was all I could bring myself to say, except that she thought Dudley was dead.

"Does Macartney think so too?" the corpse demanded.

"He worked hard enough to feel safe in thinking it," I returned bitterly, and came out with the whole story. How Macartney said the wolves had howled around the shack till their noise drove Dudley distracted, and he had slipped out after them unnoticed, with a gun; that Macartney, the two girls and half the men had gone to look for him, when he never returned, till Paulette found his wolf-doped cap torn up by the Caraquet road, and Marcia found him, in the bush—unrecognizable but for what rags of his sable-lined coat were left on his body. And Dudley's hard-boiled egg face never changed with one word of it.

"So that was how it was worked," he reflected quite composedly. "And Macartney thinks it was I Marcia found! Well, it wasn't—though I daresay it was my coat, all right, just as it was my cap Paulette picked up by the road. But it damn well would have been me, if it hadn't been for"—he paused casually, and pointed behind him—"Baker."

"Baker! That good-for-nothing devil who was always trailing after you? Why, Macartney said—" but I remembered Macartney had only said Baker was missing, too. I wheeled on the dimness of the inside cave and saw what I had missed in my flurry over Dudley. A second man—white-faced, black-eyebrowed, slim looking—was standing just where the fire glow did not reach him, staring at Paulette and me. I said, "Land of love, *Baker!*" And I may be forgiven if I swore.

Baker nodded as undramatically as Dudley. "Yes, it was me. I had sense enough all along to guess Macartney was going to finish Mr. Wilbraham with the wolf dope he'd tried out on you, if the rest of the gang hadn't. And I wouldn't stand for sculduddery like that, for one thing; and for another I thought I'd come out better in the end by sticking to the boss, like you seen me doing often enough! So I just told him he was being lain for and brought him out here. I knew this cave was safe, for I lived here two months before me and the rest of us dribbled into La Chance. And I knew the Halfway wasn't—for the two men who turned Billy Jones out of it, with a sham letter from the boss, were the two who drowned old Thompson! I've played honest in my way, Mr. Stretton, if you never thought so."

"Shut up," Dudley interrupted him indignantly. "I'd be where Marcia thought she found me, if it hadn't been for you. Listen, Stretton! I got fussy after you left for Billy Jones's that afternoon; I'd been hitting it up the day before, and you know how that leaves me! I didn't see why in blazes I hadn't gone with you to Billy's instead of sitting around the house, and a couple of hours after you left I started out to get a horse and follow you. But it's a lie that I heard wolves, or thought of them: there wasn't one around the place. Macartney wasn't around, either. I guess he was out in the bush fixing up the wolf-baited ground that was to get me, for he'd fixed up my coat and cap with it before he started. I thought something smelt like the devil when I put them on, but I never guessed it was my own things. I went out to the stable just as I might on any other day, only nobody happened to see me go, and right there I ran on Baker. I told him to come for a ride with me, but he didn't seem to think much of the horse racket; said he knew a short cut to Billy's, and it would be better for my head if we just walked. It was Baker told me the devilish reek I smelled was coming from my own coat, and I chucked it down by the stable door. God knows which of Macartney's men picked it up and wore it after I left it, for Marcia to find," even Dudley looked sick, "but it wasn't me! I smelt my cap, too, after I'd walked some of the muzziness out of me, and I threw that away—where Paulette found it. We didn't leave a sign of a track, of course; it was long before there was any snow. If I'd known why Baker had me out there, walking away from La Chance, I'd have turned back and defied Macartney, or I'd never have started. But it wasn't till it was black dark, and I'd walked enough sense into myself to ask why we were not getting to Billy Jones's, that Baker took his life in his hands—for you may bet I was fighting mad at having seemed to run away—and told me that you and I and all of us were in a trap that was going to spring and get us, and give Macartney our mine. He let out about Thompson's murder, and you and the wolf dope; and that Macartney'd kicked Billy Jones out of the Halfway with a forged dismissal from me, and had his own men waiting there to get you while he limed the bush and my cap and coat, for the wolves to get *me*. And you know I'd have been dead sure to go out after them with a gun, just as he said I did, if I'd heard them come yowling around the shack while I was in it! I'd have gone back to face Macartney, even then, only— Well, you've had experience of Macartney's wolves, and you'd know I couldn't! We could hear the row they were making even where we stood, miles away. We set off on the dead run for Caraquet and help, but we had to break the journey somewhere. We couldn't face Macartney's men at Billy's, for neither of us had a gun—and that's another lie to Macartney—and it was no good leaving the devil to run into hell. So Baker brought me here."

"But," I gasped, "I don't see how you missed me! I was here, too, that night!"

"Well, we weren't—till the morning," Dudley snapped in his old way. "It was just beginning to snow when we crawled down the burrow you'd crawled out of and found this place—and your boy."

"But I told him— D'ye mean he just *let* you find him?"

"He did not," grimly. "He was hidden away somewhere, and I don't suppose he'd ever have come out, if I hadn't happened to use what seems to have been your password! I said out loud that I'd give twenty dollars to anyone who'd get me some food; and out comes your friend, and says you told him to trust anyone who said that, and where was the twenty? So, after that, we settled down!"

"But—" Dudley's selfishness had always been colossal, yet this time it beat even me. "What did you suppose was going to become of your sister and Paulette—left with Macartney when you'd disappeared, and the Halfway picket had got *me*?" I burst out.

"My acquaintance with you made me hopeful they wouldn't get you," Dudley began drily, "and as for the girls—" but his sham indifference broke down. "Don't talk of it, will you?" he bellowed. "I did think you'd be all right, but I was in hell for those girls till I could get to Caraquet and take back help for them! Only this cursed snow stopped me. We had to wait till it was packed enough for Baker to sneak down to the Halfway and steal a couple of my own horses, for us to ride to Caraquet. But that's how I'm here—and how Marcia found a half-eaten man in my top-coat, that she thought was me!"

I was speechless. It was all so simple, even to Dudley's twenty dollars and my boy. But before I could say so, Dudley turned on me with his old vicious pounce. "Why in blazes don't you tell me what you left Marcia for, after bullying me because I did? And why are you and Paulette here, if you thought I was killed?"

"We left her because we had to, with a thousand tons of earth between us and the only way we could have got back to her alive," said I wrathfully. "And as for why we're here,"—I poured out the whole story of my return to La Chance, from Dudley's own funeral procession that met me and my bootless fight with Macartney, to the resurrection of Collins and Dunn, and Paulette's and my race across Lac Tremblant. I left out Marcia's share in my defeat, but Dudley gave a comprehending sniff.

"Marcia always was a fool about Macartney! But it's no matter, since she isn't with him—whether he's alive or dead. Only you were a worse fool, Stretton, to cross that lake with a girl in tow. I don't know why you weren't both drowned, like Thompson—" but his voice broke. He was a good little man, under his bad habits, or he never would have done what he had for Paulette. He muttered something about all the decent men who'd met their death because he wouldn't listen to Paulette when she tried to tell him the truth about Macartney, damned him up and down, and turned to Paulette with a sweet sort of roughness:

"You look done up, my girl! Here, get down by the fire and eat what our chef's got ready!" For the crippled boy had gone on with his cooking, regardless of the talk round him, and his rabbit was done.

But Paulette never looked at the food Dudley held out to her. "You're not angry, Dudley?" she asked very low. "I mean—for what I said to Nicky as we came in?"

"I was," but Dudley grinned in the half dark. "It was true enough, only nobody likes to hear their own obituary. But I knew about Stretton long ago, if you hadn't the sense to! You take him, my child, and my blessing. God knows I never asked you to marry an old soak like me!"

He shoved Paulette's hand into mine and stared at the two of us for a second. Then—"By gad," he added, in a different voice, "I hope Macartney's got drowned, or he may walk in on the lot of us!"

"How?" I demanded scornfully. "He couldn't do thirty-two miles in the time Paulette and I did fifteen, even if he knew where to do it to!"

"He doesn't have to, my young son," Dudley stood musing on it. "Baker and I didn't do any twenty, coming here; and it was Macartney's own path we came by. That doesn't go round by any Halfway! If he takes a fancy to come here by it, and strikes your tracks as you two came into Skunk's Misery, the rest wouldn't take him long! I believe—hang on a minute, while I speak to Baker!" He wheeled suddenly and disappeared into the dark of the cave where Baker stood aloof.

"You needn't worry about Macartney," I said to Paulette. "We didn't leave any tracks, once we got into broken snow!"

I turned at a rustle behind me and looked straight into the muzzle of Macartney's revolver and into Macartney's eyes!

# CHAPTER 20

## THE END

The boy at the fire let out a yelp and dropped flat. Dudley and Baker, invisible somewhere, neither spoke nor stirred. And I stood like a fool, as near the death of Nicholas Dane Stretton as ever I wish to get.

But Macartney only stood there, looking so much as usual that I guessed he must have rested outside the mouth of our burrow before he wormed down to tackle me.

"You wouldn't have left any tracks," he said, picking up what I'd just said in his everyday manner, if it had not been for the dog's grin he always wore when he was angry, "if I hadn't run on single snowshoe tracks carrying double, where you crossed the Caraquet road. And if one of you hadn't trailed your shoe tails through Skunk's Misery—that doesn't wear them!"

"How did you get here?" said I slowly, because I was calculating my spring to Macartney's gun hand.

"I walked," and I thought he had not noticed I was half a step nearer him. "If you meant me to drown myself following you over your lake, I didn't—thanks to the kind warning you made of my men. But I didn't imagine you'd drowned yourselves either—after I looked through a field glass! Charliet had plenty of snowshoes cached away; I was always quick on my feet; and after I struck your track the rest was simple—especially as you were fool enough to bring a girl here. I—" but his level voice was suddenly thick with passion. "*Get back!* If you try to grab my gun I'll shoot you, and your boy too, like dogs! You'll stay still and listen—to what I've to say. I've an account to settle with you, Stretton; now that I've cleaned up Dudley's, and he's dead!"

You could have heard a pin drop on the dead silence of that underground hole. Neither Dudley nor Baker stirred, and it hit me like a hammer that Macartney didn't know they were alive; *he didn't know!*

I stood as though I had been struck dumb; so did Paulette. Neither of us even flickered an eyelash toward the shadows behind us, where Dudley must be crouching, anything but dead, with Baker beside him. Perhaps it struck both of us, simultaneously, that Dudley had heard Macartney coming before we did and disappeared on purpose, thinking Macartney might speak naked truth to Paulette and myself, where he would have varnished it up to a mysteriously resurrected employer whom he might yet bamboozle as he always had bamboozled him. Anyhow, neither of us saw fit to give Dudley away. Macartney sneered into our silent faces.

"There's not much fight in you," he commented contemptuously. "Though it was never any good to try to fight me! If you like to have it in black and white, *I've* been all the brains of the business here—single-handed! It was I got the secret of the wolf bait from the mother of your lame friend here," he pointed with his unoccupied hand to my grovelling boy, "when first I followed Paulette out from New York and laid up in Skunk's Misery to wait till I had a clear way to get to La Chance. That old ass Thompson gave me that, when I scooped him up on the road. After I'd used him, two of my men drowned him in Lac Tremblant—and you'd never have guessed a word about it, if it hadn't been for his cursed card they overlooked in the shack here, where you found it. It was I put that bottle in your wagon the day it broke there. I did it before I knew Paulette was going to drive with you; that was the only thing in the whole business that ever gave me a scare! It was I got rid of Collins and Dunn"—I saw that he believed it, just as he believed he was rid of Dudley—"and the most of your men who might have stuck by you if it came to a fight for the mine. I had to shoot the last four of them, as you *didn't* find out that night in the assay office! I baited the bush that rid me of Dudley Wilbraham, with his yells about emeralds and hunting down Thompson's murderer; and I've got your and his mine, in spite of your blowing up and drowning all the men I meant to hold it with. But you found out most of that, even if it was a little late. What you didn't find out, or Dudley either, was that he was right about Van Ruyne's emeralds!"

Paulette leapt up like a wildcat. "You mean you took them?"

"I took them," he nodded sneeringly, and I saw her eyes blaze. "I took them—to get you into a hole you'd have to come to me to get out of!"

"But I didn't have to come to you! I—" but she spoke with sudden cutting deliberation. "I don't believe you. You were never in the Houstons' house that night. I should have seen you."

"Oh, seen me!" Macartney grinned. I think the two of them forgot me, forgot everything but that they were facing each other at last with the masks off. I know neither of them heard a slow, creeping, nearing sound in the long burrow behind Macartney, a sound that swung my blood up with the wild, furious hope that Collins and Dunn—anyhow Collins—was hot on Macartney's trail, as Macartney had been on Paulette's and mine, and was creeping down the burrow behind him now, ready to take him in the rear when I jumped at him from the front. I waited till whoever it was came close up; waited for the moment to grab Macartney, watching his triumphant, passionate eyes as he stared victoriously at Paulette.

"Seen me?" he repeated, and I hoped the sound of his own voice would deafen him to that other sound, that was so loud to me. "You saw the Houstons' guests, and their servants! You never thought of seeing the expert who was down from New York about the heating of Mrs. Houston's new orchid houses! I left the real man dead drunk in New York, in a place he wouldn't leave in a hurry; and the weekend you spent at the Houstons' I, and my plans, had the run of Mrs. Houston's library, that neither she nor anyone else ever goes into. And," he laughed outright, "it was next *your* sitting room, opening on the same upstairs balcony! I had only to put my hand through an open window to scoop Van Ruyne's emeralds out of their case while you had your back turned, writing the note you sent *outside* the case, instead of inside! Remember?" But this time he did not laugh. "I missed fire about getting you that night, thanks to that fool Wilbraham happening round with his car. But now I'll take all I did this whole business for—and that's you—Paulette Valenka!"

Paulette never took her eyes from him. "That's a lie," she said quite evenly. "Oh, not that you took the emeralds; I believe that. But it was not only to get me into trouble. It was for themselves! You had to steal something. You hadn't one penny."

"Not then!" Even in the gloom I saw two scarlet spots flare out like sealing-wax on the always dead blondeness of Macartney's cheeks. I thought I could hear his heart beat where I stood. "But I have now! With the emeralds, your late friend Dudley's mine, and *you*,"—his voice was unspeakably, insultingly significant, but that unheard rustle behind him, growing nearer, more unmistakable, kept me motionless. "By heaven, a man might call himself rich! Did you suppose Stretton here could fight me? Why, I've been the secret wolf he never had the *nous* to guess at! I—" he swung around on me like light, his revolver six inches from my ear. "Stand there," he shouted at me, "and die like Wilbraham, you—"

His hand dropped, his jaw fell with the half-spoken words in it; his eyes, all pupils, stared over my shoulder. I turned and saw Dudley—Dudley, silent, watching us both; saw him even before I grabbed the gun out of Macartney's hanging, lax hand. But Macartney never so much as felt me do it. He stared paralyzed at Dudley—little, fat, with a face like a hard-boiled egg—standing silent against the dark of the inner cave.

Dudley had a nerve when you came through to it. "I've not died, yet," he snarled out suddenly.

I had the only gun in the place and the drop on Macartney; but I never stirred. That long-heard rustle in the burrow was close on me: was—

"My God, Marcia!" said I. I never even wondered about Collins and Dunn letting her get away. Marcia stood up in the entrance from the burrow, panting, purple-faced, exhausted. Marcia sprang to Macartney—not Dudley, I doubt if she even saw Dudley—with a cry out of her very soul.

"Mack, you're not Hutton—you never took those emeralds—and for that girl! Say it's a lie, and it's *I* you love! Mack, say you love me still!"

Macartney flung back a mechanical hand and swept her away from him like a fly. She fell and lay there. None of us had said a word since Dudley came out and faced Macartney. None of us said a word now. I saw, almost indifferently, Collins burst out of the burrow behind Macartney, as Marcia had burst out, and grab me. "Stretton," he gasped, "thank God—found your tracks. But that she-devil Marcia got away from me, and—" But in his turn he jerked taut where he stood, at sight of Dudley, and stood speechless.

But I never looked at him. I looked at nothing but Macartney's face.

It was rigid, as if it were a mask that had frozen on him. The sealing-wax scarlet on his cheeks had gone out like a turned-out lamp. His eyes went from Dudley to Collins and back again, as if they were the only living part of his deathly face.

"Ah," said Macartney, "A-ah!" He dropped on the floor all in one piece, like a cut-down tree.

Collins made a plunge for him. I sent Collins reeling.

"Let him alone, you young fool," I swore. "We've got him, and he's fainted. I've seen him like this before—the night he shot our own men in the assay office. It's only his old fainting fits."

"It's his new death," said Dudley, quite quietly. He came forward and bent over Macartney, laid a hand on his breast. "Can't you see the man's gone, Stretton? It killed him: the run here—the shock of seeing me. He must have had a heart like rotten quartz!"

Paulette, Collins, Baker, all of us, stood there blankly. We had not struck a blow, or raised a voice among the whole lot of us; Macartney's gun was still warm from his grasp whence I had snatched it; and Macartney—the secret wolf at La Chance, masquerader, thief, murderer—lay dead at our feet. I heard myself say out loud: "His heart was rotten: that was why he fainted in the assay office. But— Oh, the man was mad besides! He must have been." And over my words came another voice. It was Marcia's, and it made me sick.

"Macartney," she was screaming, "Macartney!" She ran round and round like a hen in a road, before me, Dudley, all of us; then flung herself on her brother as if she had only just realized him. "You're alive—you're not dead! Can't you see he never stole any emeralds nor loved that girl, any more than he killed you? You made up lies about him, all of you! And you stand here doing nothing for him. He— Oh, Mack, speak to me! *Mack!*"

She sprang to Macartney; dropped on her knees by the dead, handsome length of him; tore open his coat and shirt. But she knelt there, rigid, with her hand on his quiet heart.

Macartney had never stolen Van Ruyne's emeralds: she had just said it. There, around Macartney's bared throat, lying on the white skin of his chest, green lights in the dull fire-glow of the cave, were Van Ruyne's emeralds, that Paulette Brown—whose real name was Tatiana Paulina Valenka—had never seen or touched since she put them back into Van Ruyne's velvet case!

I will say Marcia Wilbraham knew when she was beaten. She cowered back to Dudley and began to cry; but it was with her arms round his neck. And the fat little man held her to his heart. I turned my back sharply on the pair of them, and—my eyes met Paulette's!

There would be all sorts of fuss and unpleasantness to go through with the sheriff from Caraquet, over what was left of Macartney; there was old Thompson's death to be accounted for; Van Ruyne's emeralds to be returned to him, so that Tatiana Paulina Valenka, and not Paulette Brown, could marry that lucky, Indian-dark fool who was Nicky Stretton. There was Dudley's mine, too, all safe again, and such an incredible mine that even I would be passably rich out of it—but I barely, just barely, thought of all those things. My dream girl's blue eyes were like stars in mine, under the burnt gold of her silk-soft hair. The clear carnation rose in her cheeks as I looked at her, where she stood close to me, all mine, as I had always dreamed she would be—till I met her and was sick with doubt of it. She was mine! As far as I was concerned, this story had ended at Skunk's Misery—where it had begun, if I had only guessed it. I gave an honest start as Collins jogged my elbow.

"We can't stay here, with *that*," he whispered, nodding at Macartney. "What do you think about getting out of this? We could leave—him—here, with Baker and the boy for a guard, till we can get the Caraquet people to come and see him. We've our snowshoes, and mine and the girls', besides Macartney's, that I guess he's done with. I think we could manage along as far as the Halfway in the morning, if we made a travois of boughs for Wilbraham!"

"But," I stared at him, "Macartney's picket's there!"

"Oh, Charliet and Dunn were going to clear them out with Miss Wilbraham's rifle, while I got after her, when she broke away on to Macartney's track here," Collins returned calmly. "I expect that's all right, and they've run. Anyhow, you've got Macartney's gun! You can go ahead and see."

But I had no need to. An abandoned picket has a way of knowing when the game is up, and Macartney's men had cleared out on the double, even before Charliet's first rifle bullet missed them. We caught them afterwards, half dead in the bush—but that doesn't come in here. I walked into the Halfway with my dream girl beside me, and both of us jumped as Dudley suddenly poked his pig-eyed face between us.

"You needn't hop, you two," he commented irritably; "you can have your Old Nick, Paulette, for all me! What I'm thinking of's that boy—and Baker! I guess they saved my life all right between them, and I'm going to set them up for what's left of theirs. Got anything to say against that, hey?" with his old snarl.

"Not much," I returned soberly. But Paulette clasped both Dudley's podgy hands in hers.

"Oh, *dear* Dudley," she said softly. But there were tears in her eyes.

I know; for I kissed them away afterwards, when we were alone.